THE CHRONICLES OF ZABADUK
by JOHN WARDEN

Order this book online at www.trafford.com
or email orders@trafford.com

Most Trafford titles are also available at major online book retailers.

Illustrated by John Warden.

Note for Librarians: A cataloguing record for this book is available from Library
and Archives Canada at www.collectionscanada.ca/amicus/index-e.html

Printed in Victoria, BC, Canada.

ISBN: 978-1-4251-6488-1 (sc)
ISBN: 978-1-4251-6489-8 (e-book)

*Our mission is to efficiently provide the world's finest, most comprehensive
book publishing service, enabling every author to experience success.
To find out how to publish your book, your way, and have it available
worldwide, visit us online at www.trafford.com*

Trafford rev. 9/24/2009

www.trafford.com

North America & International
toll-free: 1 888 232 4444 (USA & Canada)
phone: 250 383 6864 ♦ fax: 812 355 4082

Table of Contents

1. Zabaduk finds his wings

"YA A A H...," EXCLAIMED ZABADUK as he slid off the back of the sofa. He found himself squeezed under its short legs with his eyes staring at the dusty wall. "I'll never get it right!" he exclaimed. He wriggled backwards and rolled underneath the sofa, and then slid his face out at the front. A buzzing met him and he peered up at a bee hovering over his nose.

"Poorrr Zabby," buzzed the bee. "When will you ever learn that you're a *snake*! Not a bee, or a bird, or a ..."

"*Dragon!*" yelled Zabaduk. "I'm a dragon! When will anybody believe me?" He glared at the bee, as far as his rather narrow eyes could manage it.

"Oh well," sighed the bee, whose name was Wuzzy, "Can't stop to argue. The queen will be cross. But try not to hurt yourself too much. Your nose is beginning to look really rather battered you know." He sped out of the French windows and was lost to sight in the garden.

Zabaduk heard a door slam, and a pattering of feet. "Hello, what's that funny thing sticking out from the sofa?" said Sammy.

"It's a dragon!" yelled Zabaduk, but of course Sammy couldn't hear him. Sammy dragged Zabaduk from the sofa, scraping his back.

"Ouch!" he cried. "Can't you be more careful?"

"He can't hear you, you know," came a gentle voice from the window. Out of the corner of his eye, Zabaduk saw a wren, looking for breadcrumbs.

"I don't care!" he shouted. "I hurt. Children don't have a proper respect for toys."

Sammy brushed the dust off Zabaduk. "Its old Zabby. How did you get there?" He coiled him carefully in a corner of the sofa. "You'll have to stay there till after Christmas. I can't take everyone to Aunt Eliza's."

"Just as well," muttered Zabaduk, though he was mollified a little by Sammy's attention.

"Oh dear," came the voice of the wren. "No more breadcrumbs for a while. Are you really a dragon? I thought dragons had wings, like us."

"I don't know what happened to them," said Zabaduk. "What's your name?"

"Wendy," replied the wren. "Perhaps you had better go to the Great Magician. He could fix you up all right."

"The Great Magician? Who is he? Could he really fix me?"

"Some of the people call him Merlin," said Wendy. "He lives in a cave at the top of the mountain. Only the birds and the rabbits know much about him. People don't really know him any more. They think he died long ago."

"How could I possibly get there?" sighed Zabaduk. "Without my wings. If I only had them back!"

"Then you wouldn't need to go," said Wendy. "I have heard people call that 'Catch 22'. I don't really know why. It's when you need something and can't get it because you need whatever it is in order to get it!"

"Yeh," said Zabaduk, "Well, I need Catch 23."

"What you need is help," said Wendy, a practical bird.

Zabaduk thought hard. And then he thought some more.

"Do you think," said Zabaduk as politely as he knew how, "Do you think ... you could ask him?"

"Ask who?" replied Wendy, not at her brightest.

"Merlin, you ... " He remembered in time that he was being polite. "The Great Magician!"

Wendy considered. "I live here, you know. I never leave the garden. I don't think my wings would go that far. I have never tried."

Zabaduk sighed again. He did a lot of sighing.

"You know," said Wendy, swallowing her last breadcrumb, "if you asked very, *very* politely, you might persuade one of the seagulls. But they are a pretty grumpy lot. Worse than you. But they do a lot of flying, can't think why."

"I've never seen a seagull," said Zabaduk. "Do they ever come here?"

"They sometimes land on the roof," said Wendy. "I don't mind asking one. They might want something in return, though."

"Oh dear," sighed Zabaduk, yet again, "another Catch 22. What could I possibly do for a seagull?"

"Nothing," said Wendy. "But – Merlin might!" Wendy was sometimes quite bright. "There is one who has lost a tail. He tends to fly around in circles a lot."

"But if he flies in circles," said Zabaduk, who was getting just a little exasperated, "how could he ever get to Merlin?"

"Well, he gets *here* somehow. I'll ask him."

Suddenly Zabaduk felt his insides stirring. It's not possible to say that his heart started beating faster, because I am not sure he had one. But a spirit he certainly had, and that was lifted. He felt a great fondness for the little wren.

"Thank you, oh thank you, Wendy," he said, and it was not politeness. The wren cocked her head on one side.

"You're very welcome," she said. "I don't know when he will come. They seem to arrive just before a storm. We'll have to wait for one."

≡≡

It grew darker as the days closed before Christmastide, and much colder. Zabaduk did not feel it, all cosy on his sofa, but there were no more crumbs for Wendy since the family had gone to Aunt Eliza's, and she did not appear on the sill. Zabaduk missed her. Then one day it grew darker than ever and the wind started to howl, shaking the window. He could see the clouds whirling past the house. He heard a loud croaking and squawking and a large white thing flapped past his vision outside.

"I wonder if it's a seagull," he thought. Then he heard a whistle.

"You there, Zabby?"

"Where else? I can only slide, and if I slide off the sofa, it's less comfy on the floor. Was that a seagull?"

"Yes, and it's the one with no tail. I think he can't keep up with the others and thinks this is far enough from the sea. I'll accost him," said the wren, who was well educated (or thought she was).

"Accost?"

"Shakespeare. It means see if he will talk to me. Bye-bye." And she flew off.

The seagull was cowering behind the chimney. Wendy tried to perch on top but the wind was too strong for her.

"Can I sit next to you?" she asked the seagull. "The wind's awfully strong up here!"

"What are you doing up here, little bird?" grunted the seagull. "Little birds like you should be looking for worms on the ground."

"I'm Wendy," she said, "and I've a favour to ask."

"Favours from a paraplegic seagull? Don't ask me to look for worms, can't stand them." He cocked his head at the wren, and relented. "I'm Breezy," he added.

"You're no paraplegic or you couldn't have got here. But how bad are you? Could you fly to the top of the mountain?"

"That mountain?" He glanced round the chimney. "Well, since I got here, I suppose I might be able to. Take me a long while, because I can only fly in circles – or coils, really, I suppose, since I gradually get forward. The height's no problem."

"I expect you mean helices," said the educated wren. "Like springs."

"That's enough of that," said Breezy. "If you can't be polite, forget it."

"Sorry," said Wendy. "I get carried away sometimes. I didn't mean to be rude."

"Carried away you will be, by the wind, if you stay here much longer. Why do you want me to fly to the mountain?"

"I have a friend called Zabaduk. He's a snake – at least he looks like a snake, but he thinks he's a dragon."

"Dragon!" gasped the seagull, cowering down. "A real one? They're dangerous. My mother said they fry birds like us with their breath and then swallow us whole!"

"Well, I don't think Zabby would do that. He's quite a little animal, and a toy. You see he thinks he lost his wings, somehow, and I told him the Great Magician might be able to grow them again. He lives in a cave on the mountain top."

"What do you know about the Great Magician? My mother used to tell me stories about him, but I have never seen him. Is he real?"

"I have never seen him because I can't reach so far and so high. As you put it, my place is near the ground, looking for worms. But I *feel*, very strongly, that he is real."

"Ouch! I was rather unkind, wasn't I? Sorry."

"That's OK," said the wren. After a pause she said slowly: "You know, he might – just might – manage to mend your tail."

There was another pause, while the seagull ruminated. (That's not Shakespeare – it's what cows do when they chew. Deep thinkers, cows.)

At length the seagull gave one of his raucous laughs.

"You're a clever little thing, aren't you? Scratch my back and I'll scratch yours. I can't really believe that Merlin – isn't that his name? – can do much about a tail that isn't there. But I like your cheek. As soon as the wind drops I'll have a go. If I ever find him, I'll see what he says – about both of us."

"You won't regret it, Breezy. I know. You're a great bird, in more ways than one. Well, I'll announce the news to Zabby and get back to my worms. Could do with a few breadcrumbs."

"Bye-bye little clown!" And the seagull crouched lower as the wren let the wind gather her and toss her like a leaf on her way to the lawn.

≡≡

Wendy tapped with her beak on the window pane.

"Zabby, Zabby!"

Zabaduk uncurled himself and looked up. "Hello Wendy, how did you get on?"

"He'll do it! He was a bit grumpy at first, hardly surprising, poor thing, but he has a sense of humour, and a good heart; and, I think, a sense of adventure. I don't think he really believes Merlin can mend his tail. What he probably likes is the challenge of getting to the mountain top."

"Wow! You're a magician yourself, Wendy."

"He is going to wait until the wind drops. Go back to sleep. I'm hungry. I can't wait till they get back from Aunt Eliza's."

"And I can't thank you enough. Have you thought of looking on the compost heap? I know they dump all kinds of food there. It may be covered by leaves, but you're so small, you could probably find a way underneath them."

"Great idea! I'll go and look now. Bye." And off she flew.

≡≡

During the night the wind dropped, but it grew colder. In the morning, Zabaduk saw through the window white spikes of frost sparkling on the grass as the sun rose, lifting the early mist. On the roof top the seagull shook out his wings and hopped to bring life to his numbed legs. He looked around at the mist and wondered if he would be able to see anything at all. But then he saw patches of pale blue sky emerging overhead. He gave a challenging roar. (It came out as a screech since his throat was still cold.) Then he flapped his wings and lifted himself off his perch. Higher and higher he rose, and then he was above the mist and could see nothing below the white cloud that covered the ground. Nothing that is – except the mountain, its rocky peak rising majestically through the mist like a beckoning finger.

The little wren tapped on the window pane, but this time Zabaduk was ready for her.

"He's off! I saw him fly up through the mist," she said.

"Can he see anything?" asked Zabaduk. "I can barely see the sun."

"Oh yes," said Wendy. "The mist is not much higher than the roof. He'll see the mountain all right. Thanks for the tip about the compost heap. I found lots of food – a whole half loaf. They must have thrown it away before leaving."

"Great," said Zabaduk. "Now we must wait again. I wish there was something I could do."

"You've done a lot for me already. Think about what you will do with your wings. Do you have any plans?"

"I've not really dared to think about it. What a disappointment if it all turns out just a dream."

"Even if it does, you can still dream of adventures. Why not start now? Then you won't be so impatient."

"All right, little mum. Don't neglect the worms and get indigestion from your loaf." Zabaduk curled up again and was lost in his thoughts as Wendy flew off in search of water. She was, indeed, feeling a bit lumpy inside.

Meanwhile the seagull aimed himself at the mountain and flew off – nearly sideways. He was not dismayed; he had a new hope, and a song in his heart. With a practised skill he dipped his right wing and rolled, coming up again facing in the other direction. There was no wind to speak of and he got himself into a rhythm, bowling along on his corkscrew flight in generally the right direction. But after some time he began to get very tired and when he looked at the mountain, it seemed just as far away as ever. Towards lunch time he began to get hungry too, and he knew that if he did not eat soon he would not have enough energy to go on.

"No fish around here, I don't suppose," he muttered to himself. "I wonder what I can find to eat." Not far off he saw some steam rising from the ground and decided to investigate. When he flew over the spot he found lorries dumping rubbish. It was still quite fresh, which was why the moisture in it was condensing into steam.

"What a horrible sight!" he said to himself, "but a good thing for gulls." Indeed he saw some of his friends tearing away at the bags with their strong beaks. "Hi Breezy!" they cried as he landed near a promising bag. "What are you up to?"

"I'm on an errand," he told them. "Off to the mountain to see the Great Magician."

"What do you want to do that for?" said his friend Croaky. "We are just filling up to get back to the sea. Better weather for fish."

"I'm hoping he can fix my tail. But I have to ask if he can put some wings on a snake who thinks he's really a dragon."

"Dragon!" they shrieked. "Why do you want to help a dragon?"

"Well he's only a toy dragon. And he's a friend of a friend. She was the one who suggested I might get my tail fixed."

"Oh ho! A girl friend. Well it's time you were thinking of settling down."

"No, no," laughed Breezy. "She's a little wren, but a plucky thing with a good heart."

At that point they all got busy eating. Breezy found some fish heads and tails in his bag, really nice and stinky. He began to feel better and drank some water from a puddle where the frost had melted.

"I must be off," he told his friends. "Long way to go."

They all looked up, shaking their heads, as he rose in the air and corkscrewed on his way. "Hope he makes it," said Croaky.

Around tea time the seagull felt his energy flagging again and took a rest on a river bank. An angler had emptied his left-over bait, a mixture of worms and tiddlers and some broken pieces of bread. He finished off the tiddlers and bread and washed them down with some cool river water. Then on he went. By nightfall the mountain began to look more like the real thing. He could make out individual rocks, and saw a deer crossing a clearing. Not far from the foot of the mountain was a farm with a warm looking barn. The great door was open and he flew in, almost colliding with the wall, but managing to settle on a rafter. He was very, *very*, tired.

Just as he was dropping off to sleep he was disturbed by a strange sounding howl – right next to him!

"Whoooo ...," said the thing. "Who are you, flying in uninvited?"

Breezy nearly fell off his perch.

"Goodness! you made me jump. Is this your home? I don't know who you are, but I am sorry to disturb you. May I rest here for a while? I am *so* tired. ... My name is Breezy, and I am a seagull," he added.

"Rather far from home, aren't you?"

"Yes, I am on an errand. I have to get to the mountain top to see the Great Magician."

"Whoooo! A bit ambitious. How do you know he will see you? He never sees anyone."

"What – no-one?" asked Breezy. "How do you know? Have you seen him?"

"I heard it from the foxes. Well, if you are so tired, you had better stay the night, if you don't mind my flying about. I need to be off for my breakfast – oh, I'm an owl if you haven't gathered already. They call me Wolly."

"Thanks, Wolly."

Poor Breezy sat wondering sadly how he was going to complete his errand, but he could not keep his eyes open and drifted off to sleep, dreaming of magicians who put spells on visitors.

It snowed in the night. Outside it was still cold, with a crust on the snow. But in the barn it was cosy. The hay in the loft above and the straw around the walls kept the inside warm. Breezy found Wolly fast asleep beside him and thought it would not be polite to wake him. He flopped quietly on to the floor and looked around, but could see nothing to eat. He hopped to the door and shivered, blinking at the glare. He heard all kinds of farmyard noises; a cock was crowing somewhere, a dog barked and the cows in the byre next door set up a chorus of moos. Then he heard a tramping of boots and hid behind the door. A boy came in whistling and wheeling a barrow. He heaved one of the bales of straw on to the barrow and looked up at the rafters.

"Hi Wolly!" he called. The owl opened one eye and glared at him.

"Go away, Billy and let me sleep," he croaked; but of course the boy couldn't understand him and went out whistling.

Breezy peered out of the doorway again. He could see some steam rising from a heap the other side of the yard. Since no-one seemed to be about he hopped his way across to investigate. Unfortunately it proved to be a heap of cow dung.

I suppose I will have to fly to find some food, he thought. He found flying difficult and tiring, so hopped whenever he could. He flapped his way up and looked around. There was another heap nearer to the farmhouse which looked more profitable. It was a compost heap. Scratching around the top he found some scraps of food and made quite a satisfying breakfast.

Well, here we go, he said to himself. Nothing venture, nothing gain.

Up in the cold morning air he could see the mountain clearly and spiralled upwards towards the summit. As he came closer, he looked out for caves, but, although there were shadows everywhere behind the rocks, none looked right. High above him was a speck in the sky which seemed to circle around the peak.

That must be an eagle, he thought. I wonder if he is dangerous! But Breezy was not really afraid. He thought he was big enough (and perhaps too salty) for the eagle to be tempted to hunt him. And his beak was almost as strong as the eagle's. There were plenty of juicy rabbits around. He had seen them darting about.

If he's local, he may know where the cave is, he thought. And his eyes are probably the best in the kingdom. Here goes, I'll ask him.

Getting near the eagle was not at all easy. Corkscrewing up and up, he grew very tired. Eventually, still some distance away, he called out:

"Hi! Can you help me?"

The eagle cocked his head and looked down. He had seen the strange bird, of course (eagles miss nothing), but decided he was not food.

"Who do you think you are, interrupting my hunting?" he whistled.

"I'm a seagull and my name is Breezy," he replied. "I'm on an errand to find the Great Magician. Do you know where his cave is?"

"I am his eyes and his claws," said the eagle, "and my task is to drive away unwanted intruders. If you are sensible you will clear off now!"

This made Breezy angry.

"I can't do that, you great bully. I am on an important errand. If I have to, I'll fight, but I can't think your master would be pleased."

Needless to say this took the great bird by surprise. Never before had he received a challenge. He was lord of the skies, and of most creatures down below.

"Brave bird," he replied. "And what is your so important errand that you question the orders of the Great Magician?"

"That is for your master, not his bodyguard!"

The eagle was too proud to lose patience, which a lesser bird might well have done after such an insult. He was, after all, Merlin's friend. He made a glide around the peak to think. Perhaps this creature, who was, indeed, being quite brave and appeared unselfish, might deserve to see Merlin.

"Stay where you are, or land on that rock," he said on his return. "And look to the West. Don't attempt to follow me, or you might find yourself a frog! I will seek out the Great Magician and let him decide."

Breezy settled in some relief on the rock and dutifully looked out to the West, where the sun was now lighting up the countryside into a wonderful view. He could see forests, and a river winding its gentle way out to the sea, a hazy line on the far horizon. He felt homesick for the sand and the waves, and his raucous friends. What was Croaky doing now, he wondered. He drifted off into sleep.

≡≡

Zabaduk was bored. It was all very well to moan about Sammy, he thought, but for all his disrespect they did have fun together. In his heart he was very fond of Sammy. He wondered what he was doing at Aunt Eliza's. He remembered her from her last visit. A small bespectacled old lady. At least he, like Sammy, thought of her as old, but really she was not so very old. She was a school teacher and knew a lot about children, and toys. In fact it was she who had given Zabaduk to Sammy last Christmas. Zabby had a distant and confused memory of a toy shop and a conversation between Aunt Eliza and the old shopkeeper. (He really was old, and Italian. He had bushy white hair and was called Giaccomo. Disrespectful people sometimes called him Jacko, but Aunt Eliza was never disrespectful.) The conversation went something like this:

"What a lovely snake," said Aunt Eliza. "He has such beautiful zigzags down his back. Hello, what are these strange lines along the top and sides?"

The shopkeeper looked carefully. "They are strange, certainly. It looks as though he may once have had wings, and a fin down his back. I wonder if he was once a dragon?"

"Look at his head!" said Aunt Eliza. "He has pointed ears! Whoever saw a snake with pointed ears? And he has a long red forked tongue all curled up in there."

"That's true," said Giaccomo. "I must look up where he came from." He walked around his counter into a back room and came back with a very worn old book. He shuffled pages around.

"Yes, I thought he might have come from there. He was made by a very special toy maker. He lives all by himself, I don't know exactly where, and sometimes takes special orders. I rather think that this must have been a reject. He sometimes sends them to me. They are not what are usually called 'rejects' – that is, they are perfectly made, but not what the person wanted. Perhaps the child was frightened of dragons, so Milo – that's what we call him, I am not sure of his real name – took off the wings. Then something must have happened. Perhaps the child died or went away and he sent the toy to me – as a snake."

"What a strange story," said Aunt Eliza. "But you have lots, I know. I would love to meet Milo. Are you sure you have no address? How do you pay him?"

"Well, you won't believe it, but he sends a bird. Usually it's a pigeon, a carrier pigeon. The pigeons bring notes or bills and take back money. But deliveries come by bigger birds – usually a pelican. Of course the toys are normally quite small animals. Sometimes he asks for things he needs, like cloth and thread instead of money."

"Could you send him a note from me," said Aunt Eliza, "asking if I could meet him?"

Giaccomo smiled. "I could try, next time a pigeon comes but, you know, he takes special care never to meet anyone."

"Do try," said Aunt Eliza. "Meanwhile I'll take the snake, or should it be drake? No that sounds silly. I wonder what Sammy will call him."

$$\equiv\Subset$$

Zabaduk shook his head and looked up as a tap came at the window.

"Hello Wendy," he said. "Any news?"

"Not really," said the wren. "But I thought I'd tell you that I met up with some seagulls going back to the sea, and they were chattering about one of their friends who was 'cracked in the head as well as the tail', who was off on some adventure."

"That has to be Breezy," said Zabaduk. "Well, we know he is on his way. Thanks for coming. I get so bored here. Why don't you bring some friends?"

"I will, next time. Bye-bye!" And off she flew.

The eagle perched on the shelf before Merlin's cave – only it was hardly a cave. There was a small plateau on the South side of the mountain, guarded by high cliffs so that it was difficult to see from most angles. Towards the inside there was a very old building which might once have been a croft or shelter for a shepherd. But this had been extended around the cliffs with wooden outbuildings. These, like the croft, were so weather-beaten that they looked like part of the mountain. Behind one of the wooden buildings a waterfall showered down the cliff, falling at the bottom onto a wheel which spun around and then flowed into a stream which ran down over the shelf to fall hundreds of feet below.

As though he had been expecting his visitor, there emerged from the croft an old man. He had long white hair and a shaggy beard, and was dressed in a black gown. Over the gown he wore a workman's apron which might once have been white, and on the front of the apron was embroidered a strange figure which could just be made out as – a dragon! The old man had spent so long alone with the birds and animals on the mountain that he could speak with them. Not only that, but (as you must have guessed) he had spent his whole life making toys, so he could speak with them too!

Merlin (for of course it was he) bowed to the eagle and spoke a greeting in a strange language, which might have once been Welsh or Gaelic, or a mixture of Celtic. It may even have included some Cornish and Breton. The eagle seemed to understand and replied.

"Master, I have seen a strange visitor, a seagull with a broken tail who claims he is on an errand to you, and wishes to meet you. He refused to go away when I tried to dissuade him, even to the point of challenging me! He is a brave bird who must have had an exhausting journey, since he flies in circles. Will you see him?"

"I have been expecting someone for a long time. I think he must be the messenger. He certainly deserves to see me, so please bring him."

The eagle bowed in return and flew off, dipping low over the edge of the shelf in a long glide, till he found an air current which lifted him in a graceful spiral up and around the peak.

Finding the sleeping seagull, he whistled:

"Wake up, sleepy head! You are honoured. The Great Magician will see you!"

"Of course he will, you monstrosity of bird life, didn't I tell you?" croaked Breezy, who was grumpy from being woken up suddenly. "Well, lead on!" He flapped his way into the air.

"I don't mind your rudeness, fish-head, but see you behave respectfully to the Great Magician, or you might well end up a frog," replied the eagle, whose name was Whirlwind. He led the way round the mountain and landed gracefully on Merlin's shelf. Breezy clumped down behind him.

Merlin was waiting for them. Seeing the eagle bowing respectfully, Breezy tried to copy him, but being less practised, nearly fell over.

"Welcome, my friend," said the Great Magician to Breezy. "I understand you have come on an errand. Come inside with me and I will see what can be done. Thank you Whirlwind. Go and catch your lunch. You might find something for us too."

As the eagle flew off, Breezy hopped behind Merlin into the croft. Breezy looked around him, filled with curiosity and expecting all kinds of magical apparatus. But the shelves were full of toys! What kind of magician is this, he thought.

"I expect you are hungry and thirsty," said Merlin. Whirlwind will bring us something for lunch, I'm sure, but here are some crusts from my breakfast and some water."

Breezy ate and drank gratefully. Merlin waited until he had finished.

"Now tell me your story," he said. So Breezy told him all about the little wren, and Zabaduk, and Sammy, and Aunt Eliza and, finally, about his tail.

"Well, well, well," said Merlin at the end. Truth to tell his name was not really Merlin, any more than he was really a magician. Although not Italian, he became known in Italy (where the best toys used to be made) as Orlando da Milano, which is a bit of a mouthful. He became known by humans as Milo, and by the toys and animals as Merlin. He may not have been a magician, but he was certainly a magical person.

"I had better do some explaining," he continued. "I have a very good friend called Giaccomo, or Jacky for short, who owns a toy shop and I regularly send him toys to sell. Sometimes he sends me special orders. One of these was for a dragon. I have a special fondness for dragons, because I am a Celt and dragons used to live in the Celtic lands long ago. The dragon is still the emblem of Wales – where you can see I picked up my apron, again long ago, but not as long ago as the dragons.

"Anyway I made a beautiful dragon and sent it off. To my dismay, my pelican – who delivers for me – was attacked! You see I have an enemy called Maladok who also makes toys, but does not have all my secrets. *My* toys can speak to the birds and animals and, of course, to me. Maladok will stop at nothing to get this secret and thinks (he is quite wrong of course) that he can find out by experimenting with my toys, which he steals when he can. He will never find out because he lives in a town and does not love the creatures around him (mostly humans) or the toys he makes. It has taken me a great deal of love, and most of my life. Which is why I live up here, away from humankind. I am not sure that I can still speak to humans; perhaps to a real Celt or an Italian.

"Maladok started by taking off the dragon's wings and his dorsal fin – the one running along his back. And his legs. Before he could do any more damage, one of my spotter birds – a kite – saw what he was about and told me. That's when Whirlwind is really useful. He flew right into Maladok's workshop, snatched up Zabaduk (for of course it was him) and brought him to Giaccomo. But neither Whirlwind nor Giaccomo realised what had happened to Zabaduk. Giaccomo saw that he was damaged, which surprised him a bit, but mended him, and much later he must have sold him to Aunt Eliza. Giaccomo's memory is not what it was. He must have forgotten mending him."

This was a very long story for Breezy, who had not a very big brain.

"I wonder how much of all that you can remember," said Merlin doubtfully. "Never mind, I will have to write a note anyway. It had better be to Giaccomo. My Italian is better than my English."

Breezy, however, was awe-struck, and had lots of questions.

"Who attacked the pelican?" was his first. "What kind of birds are Maladok's friends? How does he talk to them?"

"He doesn't talk to them," said Merlin. "He trains them – falcons. They are not friends, they are slaves. He thinks that I do the same – at least, in his heart he must know that I talk to my friends, but it makes him so jealous he conveniently forgets it."

"But how did he find the pelican?"

"Portia – my best pelican is Portia. Poor Portia, she was so sad and ashamed, but it was not her fault. The falcon – Flash, I think he was, dived at her eye. She rolled over to avoid him and Zabaduk fell out of her beak. You see, she couldn't close it properly because he was bigger than most of my toys, and stuck out. Flash dived straight down and picked him up in his claws. Falcons are very quick."

"Do you have any seagull friends?"

"No, you are my first!"

Breezy shook his feathers in pride, and tried another bow, more successfully this time. Merlin smiled and bowed back.

"Will you be able to give Zabby new wings?" he asked

"Of course I will. I was waiting to hear where he was, but you did my work for me, or you and Wendy together. I am sorry not to be able to thank her. Do you think there is anything she needs?"

Breezy thought. "I can't think of anything she needs. She is a bright and friendly bird, and rather adventurous. What she would love best, I think, would be to meet you."

"Hmm, not so easy. Perhaps Portia could bring her, if she could trust her not to swallow! Not of course that she ever would."

"Brilliant!" said Breezy. "I think she would love it."

"And what about you?" asked Merlin, at last.

"Oh, my tail," said Breezy bashfully.

"How did you come to lose it?"

"My nest was attacked when I was little. Some big bird or other. I just remember his terrible eye and huge curved beak. He picked me up by the tail and it fell off. I'm only young still, you know. Luckily (for me) the bird chose one of my brothers and left me on the ground. My mother came back and rescued me – but without my tail."

"I wonder if it was one of Maladok's falcons," said Merlin. "Rather a coincidence, but I have never believed in coincidences. Every action changes the world at the same moment. I think it must have been at the same moment Flash attacked Portia." He thought for a while.

"I'm really only a toy maker, you know. But let me have a close look. Here, hop on this table"

Breezy hopped closer and flapped on to the table, turning his back politely.

"Hmm, yes, as I thought. You are still young enough that

new feathers are beginning to come through. You can't see them because they are behind you, but in – probably a year – they should be long enough to be a real help. I know it's an awful wait. Perhaps I can do something temporary. I have, after all, made lots of toy birds! Do you mind losing a few wing feathers? They will grow back too."

Breezy was a bit reluctant, but his faith in Merlin was now complete. "OK," he said," shaking his feathers again – not for the last time, I hope, he thought.

"Here we go," said Merlin. "It will hurt a bit. No pain, no gain. Rather like the dentist, but you are spared them at least." And he gave a sharp tug to one of Breezy's longest feathers. He went on, with poor Breezy shuddering, until he had a good bunch.

"Now, superglue, I think. My own special brand. This is where I get my reputation. The great difficulty is to avoid spoiling your new feathers. That would never do"

With the most tremendous care, Merlin separated the fine fluffy new feathers and suddenly jabbed a big feather into Breezy's skin.

"Ouch!" gasped the seagull. But Merlin was so skilful, and the dab of glue on the end of the feather so immediately strong, that the skin was not pierced. He only made a hollow, so narrow that the sides stuck to the end of the feather.

"Excellent, if I say so myself," said Merlin. He went on until all the big feathers were in place.

"Now, try a little shake."

Breezy was by this time gasping with the effort of keeping still while being continuously pricked, and was only too pleased to oblige. Shaking his new tail was quite an experience and he made a bit of a mess of it. As with his first bow he tumbled right over.

Merlin laughed. "Takes a bit of getting used to," he said. See if you can fly straight towards the cliff edge. Just a bit at a time."

Breezy mentally crossed his toes, took a deep breath, and

launched himself. He went so fast that he was over the edge of the cliff before he knew what had happened. He panicked, finding himself plummeting down.

"Just like a fledgling," he said in disgust. He spread his wings and went into a gliding swoop. Suddenly he saw that he was looking straight ahead.

"Wow-eee!" he cried. He tried a gentle curve to the left and saw the horizon moving slowly round. "I can fly! I can fly!" he cried. He began to flap his wings. At first it felt awkward to manage his tail and his wings at the same time. It took more effort to climb since he had lost a lot of feathers. He had to flap a little faster. But in no time, it seemed, he found what he had to do. He flew up over the summit where Whirlwind was circling, looking down at him.

"What, no more corkscrews?" called the great bird.

"I can fly! I can fly!" he shouted back. "What a great man he is. He said he wasn't a magician, but I know better."

"All depends how you look at it," said Whirlwind. "I am no one's servant, but to help him is simply a pleasure."

"Yes, I can understand," replied Breezy. "Better go and thank him." He executed a graceful downward swoop around the peak and landed with a slide on the plateau. Merlin was there watching his antics.

"Oh thank you, thank you," said Breezy. "It's wonderful!"

"Yes, better than I expected," replied Merlin. "It's amazing how nature will adapt. Well now. Come in again. I have a letter that needs to be delivered. Can you manage that?"

"My great pleasure, said Breezy. "Anything you like!" He hopped in after the great man.

"This is to go to Giaccomo. It explains what has happened and what I intend to do. I will send Portia to fetch Zabaduk. Hopefully I can have him back in time for Sammy's return but in case something should happen, he and his parents, and Aunt Eliza, had better know the whole story. As soon as you have delivered the letter, go and find Wendy. I hope between the three of you, you can find a way in for Portia. It may be difficult. I will send her in three days time. Then you can fly back here with them, if you like. I will be sending Whirlwind as bodyguard. Even you might not be a match for Flash, and I don't want to lose Zabaduk again."

"No need for Whirlwind!" said Breezy. "I can deal with any old falcon!"

Merlin smiled. "I believe you," he said. "We'll see. Here's the letter, but I must explain how to find Giaccomo. He lives in a little house at the edge of the town not far from Sammy's place. It looks just like a doll's house and has a big sleigh in the front garden. The children think it's used by Father Christmas."

"I'll find it," said Breezy. "Goodbye, and thank you again."

And off he flew.

≡≋≡

Zabaduk woke up again as the little wren tapped on the window. This time there were two birds there. One was a huge seagull – at least he seemed huge next to Wendy.

"This is Breezy," said Wendy, "and you know what – he has a new tail! Breezy, meet Zabaduk."

Breezy bowed. He was getting quite good at it. Zabby tried to bow in return but could only manage a wriggle.

"Congratulations!" he said. "Did you find out about my wings?"

"Yes he certainly did," said Wendy, who was obviously in charge. "Merlin is going to fix you up, very soon. A pelican is coming to fetch you."

"Goodness! A pelican?"

"Yes a lady pelican called Portia. And I am invited to meet the Great Magician!"

"Oh, I am so glad," said Zabaduk. "You certainly deserve to."

"I only wish I could go with you," said the wren. "But I will have to go later when Portia has time."

The seagull coughed – at least it was a sort of polite grunt.

"I don't suppose you would dare to ride on my back?" he offered.

Wendy jumped up and down. "Do you really think you could carry me?" she said.

"Well you are much lighter than a fish," said Breezy. "I have carried lots of them – in my beak of course. But you would have to hang on really tight."

"Oh, I am sure I could do that," replied Wendy. "Anyway I am a bird, you know, even if I am small. If I fell off, I would simply fly down – or land on you again if you could fly underneath me."

"That's true," said Breezy.

"Now, how is the pelican to get in and out?" continued the Wren.

Zabaduk thought. "I know, there is a cat, Molly. She has a cat flap to get in and out. I will try to persuade her to open it so that I can slide out."

"I know that cat!" said Wendy. "I wouldn't trust her an inch."

At the sound of her name a large tabby cat uncurled from the armchair where she was sleeping, looked at the birds on the windowsill and growled.

"Molly! These are my very good friends. Just you behave or I will chase you when I have my wings. Who knows, I might even be able to breathe fire!"

"Wings indeed! Just who do you think you are, snaky?"

"I'm really a dragon. *Really*, you know. The Great Magician is going to give me back wings!"

Molly looked doubtful. "The Great Magician is real?"

"Of course he is. How do you think my friend Breezy got his tail back? Breezy is the seagull. I shouldn't try attacking him if I were you. And he's my friend, and Wendy's, so you can leave her alone, too."

"Anything you say," sighed Molly, who was a lazy creature. She was really quite soft hearted, though she had to put on a fierce face sometimes to keep her self-respect in front of birds. She wandered over to the window. Wendy grew a bit agitated, but Molly said:

"Don't be afraid, little bird. Any friend of Zabby's is a friend of mine. How do you do? Welcome to you both."

The birds relaxed. Zabaduk explained what they needed.

"No problem," said Molly. "If you get stuck I can always pull you out."

"The pelican should be here tomorrow," said Breezy. "I will explain to her that you are friendly. Though I imagine she is big enough not to worry too much. Bye-bye, then. See you both tomorrow."

※

Next morning they waited together on the windowsill. They waited and waited. Finally Breezy said "She must be lost. I will go and see if I can find her."

It was cloudy and rather dark. There might be more snow coming, he thought. He hovered around just beneath the clouds. Nothing. Then he went up through them. There it was really gloomy, with very few breaks. Suddenly, in one of them, he thought he saw a flash of white disappearing into the gloom. He chased after it crying "Portia, Portia!" He was flying so fast that he banged right into her! They tumbled down through the clouds in a whirl of feathers and finally managed to glide apart as they broke through the bottom.

"Goodness gracious, you daft bird, can't you see where you are going?" gasped Portia – for it was her, luckily, and not an angry eagle.

"Sorry, so sorry," replied Breezy, "I really couldn't. Why are you flying up here? You could never find us."

"I was chased!" said Portia. "Flash is up there somewhere. I had to hide to avoid showing him where I was going. Then of course I got lost. Hopefully, so is he."

"Well, we're right over the house," said Breezy, "come on, follow me as quickly as you can." He dived down straight at the house, zooming around to the cat flap. But Portia was not quite so fast. Just before she arrived a black speck emerged. Neither of them saw it, but Wendy did. She too was flying about trying to spot Breezy.

That does not look good, she said to herself. Like all small birds she could tell a falcon by its shape a long way off. I wonder if he saw Portia? But the falcon was making large circles, searching. Wendy flew back to the cat flap.

There she found the flap held open by the pelican's beak and Zabaduk wriggling through. Breezy was on the roof, keeping a lookout in his shelter behind the chimney. She perched on the gutter.

"Flash is up there, below the clouds, but I don't think he saw you," she told them.

"Oh dear," sighed Portia, who was a long-suffering, motherly bird. "However are we going to avoid him?"

"I'll go and entice him," said the brave Wendy. "I expect he is hungry by now and disappointed to have missed you."

"No, no, no!" gasped Portia. "You will be killed!"

"Oh no I won't," replied the little wren. "I have met falcons before now. They are really quite silly birds. Once they have made up their minds they can't change direction quickly. I will fly towards the woods, not too high, and zoom into them when I see him dive. As soon as you see him follow me, get up into the clouds as fast as you can. Can you hear me?" she called out to Breezy. "Give them the signal!"

"OK," said Breezy, "but for heaven's sake be careful!"

Zabaduk, by now, had managed to wriggle through. Portia picked him up gently. "Make yourself as comfortable as you can," she said. Zabaduk managed to curl around so that only his head stuck out in front. The top of Portia's beak rested lightly behind his ears.

"I'm fine," he said. "Ready!"

The wren darted up towards the falcon while Breezy kept his eye on them. Wendy flew as close as she dared to Flash and then pretended to notice him, turning sharply to catch his attention. The falcon seemed to hesitate and then followed swiftly and dived before the smaller birds expected it. Breezy launched himself into the air, squawking madly, and Flash turned in mid air to look, allowing Wendy to dart into the wood. Meanwhile Portia and Zabaduk reached the clouds and disappeared.

But Flash was furious at having lost his lunch. He turned to Breezy giving a loud challenge and flew at him. Breezy was more scared than he expected, seeing the long wings and vicious hooked beak, and the angry eyes staring at him. He turned at an angle, forcing the falcon to turn after him, and climbed. The birds went spiralling up together.

Then Breezy remembered his own beak, and his great voice. "This won't do," he thought. Having now the advantage of height, he decided to try some falcon tricks. He gave an almighty shriek and dived at Flash. The falcon was taken completely by surprise, sitting on his tail and flapping his wings fast. Breezy took a peck at his head as he swept past and found some feathers in his beak. Flash was angrier still, but he was scared too. He was really a bully, going for small birds and young rabbits that could not fight back. Never had any bird *ever* dared to attack him! He flew over Breezy and prepared to dive. But he was half-hearted. Meanwhile Breezy found himself over the wood.

The others must have got away by now, he thought. Time to finish this scrap. He dived into the wood. The falcon could not follow him there; he was a bird of the upper air. He circled round for a while and then flew off in his search for Portia.

"Wendy! Where are you?" called Breezy

"Here I am, I was watching you," she replied. "What a fight! You were terrific!"

"I don't know about that," shrugged Breezy. "He had me pretty scared."

"You ended it at exactly the right time," said Wendy. "The others are well away. Keeping your head is as important as bravery. It would have been terrible for all of us if you had lost. Now we must try to find them before Flash can. Sooner or later he will realise that they are on the way to the mountain. Don't forget you are supposed to be the bodyguard. Ready for me?"

Breezy found himself wondering what would happen if there was another fight when he had Wendy on his back. Too late to worry now, he thought. I can't disappoint Wendy, after she was so brave.

Wendy hopped on his back, sliding her little legs around his neck like a horseman and tangling her claws in his feathers. "Off you go," she cried happily.

<hr />

"Can you find the way in all this cloud?" asked Zabaduk.

"Not really sure," replied Portia. "When I'm a bit nearer I can sometimes smell my way – at least something tells me where the mountain is. But we are too far off. I will have to drop down and see where we are."

They glided down until they could see the ground below.

"Now I know," she said and made a slight correction. They flew slowly on. Portia was a big heavy bird and had quite a weight to carry. "I think we will have to go on like this and see if we can make Wolly's place before nightfall," she said. "It's a long way." On they went.

Meanwhile Breezy, with Wendy enjoying her ride, was trying to catch up. He could not see the mountain, but knew the way quite well by this time. Wendy was so light she was not really a burden and they made a good speed.

"We should catch them up in an hour or so," said Breezy. "How are you doing?"

"Having the time of my life!" said Wendy. "What a view! I have never been so high, even if we are under the clouds."

"I think they will be making for the barn," said Breezy. It's too far to the mountain today at their speed. I hope Flash won't find us."

They caught up with Portia as it was getting darker and snow was now beginning to fall.

"I am getting really tired," she said when they reached her, "and I don't like this snow. I feel heavier and heavier."

"Look, there's a farm, right ahead," cried Wendy, as loudly as she could. She had the best view of all. "Is that the barn where Wolly lives?"

"Yes," replied Breezy and called: "There's the barn! Can you make it?"

"I hope so," gasped Portia.

And they did, just. When they entered the barn she was covered in snow. Wendy had a little white hat, but Breezy's wings were moving so fast that the snow did not settle.

"Portia, goodness me," came Wolly's voice. "You look like a snowbird. And who's that in your beak?"

"Zabaduk, meet Wolly," she replied, dropping him on the floor. Zabaduk looked up at Wolly and did his wriggle.

"I hope you don't mind this intrusion," he said politely.

"Any friend of Portia's is a friend of mine. You must be the wingless dragon Breezy was telling me about. And here's the bird himself. Who's your friend?"

"This is Wendy. A very brave wren."

"Hello," said Wendy. "So pleased to meet you, Wolly. I know all about you from Breezy."

"Sounds as thought you have all had some adventures," said Wolly. "You must tell me all about it."

"Water first," said Portia. "I'm so thirsty. I wonder if there is any food anywhere?"

"There's a water trough in the yard," said Wolly. "And do you know, Whirlwind brought in your dinner! I was never so surprised. Gave me a terrible shock to wake up suddenly with that huge bird in front of me. I thought my last moment had come. The Great Magician must have thought you would arrive here hungry. Its all hidden upstairs in the hay store. The cowmen won't need to get in there tonight, but may arrive here any time. Hurry and get your drinks and I'll join you."

Soon they were upstairs, through the trap door, and settled in the hay having a feast, all except Zabaduk, who didn't need food or drink.

"Just as well," he told them, "or I might eat you all!"

⇒⇐

After a good night's rest they were up at first light. Snow covered the ground, but the dawn was crisp and cool and the mountain in full view. The birds took off together and climbed towards the peak with Breezy above and behind. But as they approached there was a whistling noise.

"Look out!" screamed Wendy. The falcon was headed straight for her. Suddenly there was another flurry of wings and the shadow of a huge bird covered her. Flash seemed to be picked up just before his stretched-out talons could grab her. They watched as Whirlwind soared up grasping Flash in his even bigger talons.

"Follow me!" he cried. "The Great Magician will know what to do with him." And he was away, up and around the peak.

By the time they reached the plateau Whirlwind was settled on the ground in front of the croft with his foot on a very frightened Flash. Merlin stood in front of them, hands on hips. The other birds landed a little way off and watched the drama.

"Well done, Whirlwind, well done indeed. I knew I could rely on you. Now we have the culprit, and perhaps the trouble will cease – at least for a while."

The falcon, squashed as he was, gave a squawk.

"Can you really talk to us?" he gurgled, "I thought it was all a lie."

"There's a lot you don't know, serving a master like Maladok," said Whirlwind, lifting his foot a little.

"What choice have I had?" replied Flash. "Besides he has always treated me well. I have a great deal of freedom – unlike many I know, stuck in cages."

"But you are still his slave," said Merlin. "Would you like to be free?"

"How do I know? I know no other life. He has been my master since I was born. What is this freedom?"

"Yes. I can see it will be difficult for me to explain. You have to understand love before you can understand freedom. My friends love me. They stay near me because it is their joy. If they wish, they can fly away. Sometimes they do. Just to see that they can. They come and go as they please. But I have never known anyone who never returned."

"Do I not love my master?" asked Flash in a puzzled voice. "I always return to him."

"You return because it is all you know. It is your whole life. Have you ever had a friend – a real friend, or a mate?"

"There are other falcons like me, and the dogs."

"The falcons are like you. They know only death and destruction. And the dogs, I can imagine, are chained watch dogs. Are they ever friendly with other people or animals? Do you or the other falcons ever make friends with others?"

Flash said nothing. He was sad and ashamed. He had been defeated for the first time in his life. Something deep inside was telling him he must return to his master. But something else was asking – must this be for always?

"There is only one thing I can think of that might change you," said Merlin. "You need to find a mate." He went to the very edge of the plateau, put his fingers in his mouth and gave a piercing whistle. Although there were no mountains around, it was so loud and long it seemed to be echoed by the clouds. They all waited.

In a minute a speck could be seen high up among the clouds. It was joined by another, and another. Soon a whole flock of long-winged birds could be seen circling above. His friends watched in awe as they came lower and lower. Finally a family of red kites settled on the rim of the plateau, while yet others hovered overhead. At a gesture from Merlin, Whirlwind released Flash who looked at the kites in a puzzled way.

Merlin addressed the mother kite.

"Welcome Kitty. Good to see you all again. I would like you to meet Flash. He has had a difficult life as a slave. He needs a mate. Can you help?"

Kitty looked around at her brood. "I don't know if any of mine would care to mate with a falcon. They are killers. You know we never kill."

"That is why I have asked you. Flash knows nothing but killing. It's time he learned. What he needs is love."

One of the kites, the smallest and scruffiest, was looking at Flash rather bashfully. Wendy was quick to notice. She was always the brightest. She hopped quietly up to Flash (a particularly brave thing to do for such a wee bird). She whispered to him:

"Look at the little one. I think she likes you."

Very surprised, Flash turned to look at her, remembering chasing her to the wood, and his last dive at her. Wonders will never cease, he thought. Then turned to look closely at the kite. He had the strangest feeling. That poor bird, he thought, must be a runt. She knows she is unlikely ever to attract a mate. She may not even be able to fly properly. Like me, she needs someone to look after her, to be with. Is this what they call love?

"Is it polite to talk to her?" he whispered to Wendy.

Wendy flew on to Merlin's shoulder, which seemed to delight him.

"You must be Wendy," he said smiling. "If I ever gave medals, you would certainly have one! What can I do for you?"

Wendy whispered in his ear.

"I think the small kite and Flash would like to meet, but they don't know how."

"Then I had better introduce them," said Merlin. "Hop down for a minute." Wendy flew down, and Merlin approached Flash. He stretched his arm out for Flash to sit on. "Would you come with me for a moment?" he asked gently.

Flash hesitated. "Nothing venture, nothing gain," he thought and hopped on to Merlin's forearm which had some protection from his claws. Merlin lifted him up and addressed the kites.

"Kitty, I don't know the name of your smallest. Would you ask her if she would care to meet Flash?"

Kitty looked very doubtful but, trusting Merlin, she turned to the small kite.

"Candy, what do you think?"

"Come, Candy," called Merlin and extended his other arm. His smile was so loving that Candy couldn't resist him. But she also wanted to meet Flash. He was so exactly like her dreams – a big strong bird who would defend her and never laugh at her like her brothers. She flew on to Merlin's arm.

Merlin brought his arms slowly closer, letting the birds inspect each other.

"Candy meet Flash; Flash meet Candy."

The birds bowed silently to each other. It seemed the natural thing to do. Flash found his voice eventually.

"Would you really be my mate?" he asked. "They may not have told you enough. I am – I was – maybe I still am – Maladok's slave. But I think, if you accepted, I would be free of him."

"You probably don't know enough about me," replied the kite. "I have always been the clumsy one of the family. My legs and wings are not as strong as the others."

"So we will never laugh at each other, that is, laugh in an unfriendly way," said Flash. "We are the misfits."

"Of course we won't," said Candy, delightedly. "And of course I will be your mate, if you will defend me."

Flash lifted himself to his full height and stared at everyone, one at a time (except for Merlin whose face was above him). "Just let them dare mistreat you!" he replied. "Just let them dare!"

"You may kiss the bride," laughed Merlin and brought his arms together. Candy hopped on to his other arm and nuzzled Flash, who was now looking very proud.

"What a day," said Merlin. "Off you both hop, my arm is getting tired. I'm only an old toy maker, remember. Kitty, you will need to guide the young couple a bit. Flash knows nothing about nesting."

"But I do!" announced Candy. "Come with me!" She had had enough of her family (for the time being). And they flew off together.

Kitty looked after her rather sadly. "It's for the best," she murmured. "But I will miss her. For all her clumsiness, she is – was – the brightest and bravest. Flash has made a good choice."

"Well, my friends," said Merlin. "I must be about my business. Zabaduk, you may not remember me, but it's wonderful to see you again. Come with me to my workshop and we'll see about some wings for you.

"Whirlwind, some supper would be very welcome. If you can

find Flash, he might be persuaded to give you a hand. No, on second thoughts, he had better not do any more killing for a while. Wendy and Breezy, you great birds, why don't you tell the kites all about your adventures!"

He gathered up Zabaduk and walked off to his workshop.

The workshop turned out to be one of the outbuildings. When Merlin deposited him on the central table, Zabaduk looked around curiously. All around were shelves full of the strangest tools, rolls of cloth, leather-bound books, and unfinished toys. Merlin saw him looking at them.

"I get stuck sometimes," he said. "Then I have to put them down until something – or someone – tells me what to do next. I hope I don't get stuck with you. There is not much time if we are to get you back before Sammy returns. Now, let me see, can I remember what the wings were like."

He searched around among the bales of cloth.

"Yes, here we are, my special 'cloth of gold'." He then went to one of the old books and inspected a picture.

"This is going to take a long time," he told Zabaduk. "Several days. You will have to be patient, or go to sleep while I prepare the wings."

But Zabaduk was far too curious to sleep. He watched while Merlin unfolded the cloth, spread it out and drew on it, and then started cutting it with one of his tools. He then searched for and found other colours.

When he had cut out all the patterns, it was growing dark and difficult to see. Leaving the unfinished work on the table he went out for a walk and then sat at the edge of the plateau for a long time, watching the final colours of the sunset in the sky. The evening star glowed above the horizon. Zabaduk watched him as birds and animals gathered around him and seemed to murmur to him and each other in soft voices, Breezy and Wendy among them. Wendy cheekily found a perch on Merlin's shoulder. Whirlwind settled on a rock and seemed to guard them all. There was swish and a soft "Woooh.." and Wolly arrived. "Quite a conference," thought Zabaduk, "or perhaps an ancient ritual. Evensong." When it was quite dark they went away in small groups. Breezy and Wendy sneaked into the croft, hoping Merlin would not mind. It was by now very cold.

Merlin came in shivering. "A lovely evening," he said, rubbing his hands by the fire, "but cold for my old bones. Come on Zabaduk. Time for me at least to eat." He picked him up and carried over to the croft, where he put more wood on the fire. Whirlwind had left a dead rabbit and flown off to his own meal.

"I'm sorry if this offends you," he said to Zabaduk, "but I must live like my ancestors, and take my part in the balance of nature. Rabbit stew and nettle soup." He put some nettles from a pile in the corner into a pot and hung it on the fire to boil, while he skinned and cut up the rabbit. While the rabbit stewed he went out and returned with a bottle.

"Merlin's special blend, five years old. We must toast your re-emergence." He opened the bottle, filled a mug and raised it to Zabaduk. "Here's to a happy future!" He drank deeply. "A goodly year," he said.

After supper he curled up on some blankets near the fire and they all went to sleep.

∌⋵

Next day Merlin and Zabaduk said their farewells to Breezy and Wendy and saw them off on their journey home. The days went by and the wings, and the fin and legs took shape. Dragon's wings are not like bird's wings. They are quite thin, like a bat's, with the membranes divided up by springy ribs; very tricky to make. Merlin made the ribs from long pieces of split bone, perhaps from a heron's legs. These were covered with silky material and stiffened and strengthened with a waterproofing liquid which dried very shiny. There came at last a moment when they were ready for fitting.

"Now, my friend," said Merlin, arranging Zabaduk on the table, "you must go to sleep. When you wake up you will be the dragon you used to be – or better, I hope." He laid his hands gently on him and Zabaduk found himself getting very sleepy. When he was quite still, Merlin undid Giaccomo's seams and fitted the new limbs. This was a difficult operation, since the wings were connected with cunning springs which allowed them to furl and unfurl and even to flap in a jerky way. Similar springs were fitted to the short legs, allowing them to walk. When Merlin had finished, he seemed to give a blessing and then carried him out into the sunlight to awaken.

As the sun worked its own magic, Zabaduk gradually woke. He found himself staring out at the view over the countryside. A voice behind him said, "Open your wings, little dragon." Still a little woozy, Zabaduk felt a strange weight and stiffness in his shoulders. He found he could move them. With a sudden snap part of them lifted. There was another snap and suddenly he knew his wings were open. He turned his head and looked at them in amazement. He was frightened and turned around to look at Merlin, and then found his feet moving!

"What should I do?" he asked, trembling.

"Why, what should you do but fly, Zabby. Fly into the house!"

Zabaduk took a deep breath and – flapped his wings! He found himself rising in the air, dipped forward and flew into the croft, landing rather heavily on the table.

"I'm a *dragon!*" He yelled in joy.

Soon, amazingly soon considering he was reborn, he was flying around the croft, and then out into the air.

"While you are with me, you can fly when you like, but not too far from the plateau, at least during the day. You must not be seen by humans. But when you are home, you must only fly at night, when all humans are asleep. You will find you can't fly by day. It would be too dangerous for me to let you. If they saw you, my gift might be lost. Toys for them never move on their own, or talk. They can't understand your kind of talk, so that's not a danger, but if they saw you fly – well, I don't know what would happen, but it never must!"

"I don't mind. In fact I quite understand," said Zabaduk. "What matters is that I *know* I'm a proper dragon. And Sammy will know, too. He would not expect me to fly."

"Now let's see about getting you back home and into the house. I asked Breezy and Portia to come back after a week. I don't think we can leave you to fly home alone, and at night. You will have to suffer Portia's beak again, I think. But you are now much bigger. I hope she can still manage. They should be here tomorrow. Do you think between the three of you, you could open the cat flap?"

"I am sure we could. Portia managed to hold it open last time. But could I not fly too, part of the way? We would be right up high, if the weather holds. And I could rest on her back, perhaps."

Merlin considered. "Yes. That might even be best. But be sure you never get too tired and have to descend. Keep very close to Portia."

"I never thought I would want to leave. Being here, staying with you, has been so special. But suddenly I do. I miss Sammy."

"That's only natural, and good. Children and their toys need to be together. So, this is our last night together. Is there anything special you would like to do?"

"Would Whirlwind consider taking me for a trip?" asked Zabaduk. "A training exercise?"

"Good idea, let's see," replied Merlin and he went outside and whistled. Soon the great bird swooped down. They bowed to each other.

"Would you be so kind as to accompany my friend Zabby on a little trip? He has to go home tomorrow. Its a long way to go. He will have to fly part of the way, and needs some practice."

"It would give me great pleasure. He looks quite splendid. I can imagine we will attract some attention."

"So long as it's up in the air!" said Merlin. "Don't be too long. I think half an hour would be plenty."

"Come, little dragon," said the great bird and dived off the edge of the plateau. Zabaduk took off and followed him down in a great dive. They swooped up to the left and climbed up and around the peak. Who should they meet there but the kites.

"Hello, who's that?" called Kitty. "Not the little toy snake I saw?"

"This is my friend Zabaduk," replied Whirlwind. "He's a dragon! So treat him with respect."

"No offence," said Kitty hurriedly.

"That's all right," said Zabaduk. "I did look like a snake. It used to make me cross. But no longer. Merlin gave me back my wings!"

"Well, you are a wonderful sight," said Kitty. "We are all delighted to meet you – and look who's coming!" It was Flash and Candy. Flash kept his distance. He was still a bit ashamed of kidnapping Zabaduk, but Candy swooped down at him, playfully. "Catch me if you can," she cried.

Zabaduk dodged her, and then chased her down and around the flock. "Careful," he cried, "or I will burn you up!"

"Oh yeah! Just you try." Others of the fledglings joined in and they chased each other round the peak while Whirlwind and Kitty looked on from above, smiling. Quite soon Zabaduk grew very tired. Whirlwind saw him beginning to lose height and called out:

"That's enough for now, Zabaduk. Time to go home. Just open your wings and glide down." Zabaduk was thankful to do so.

"Goodbye, all of you," he called. "See you sometime. Come and visit us!" He turned and glided down to the plateau where Merlin stood watching.

"Thank you so much, Whirlwind. I did so enjoy that," he called to the circling bird.

"My great pleasure," was the reply. "I loved watching you. I have never seen a dragon fly. Quite an experience. Kitty and the others were very impressed." And off he flew.

Zabaduk enjoyed his last evensong. I think I will miss that the most, he thought.

The journey home was relatively uneventful. One surprise was that Flash and Candy joined them for the trip, Candy to see where Zabaduk came from, and Flash to fly bodyguard. Certainly no-one attacked them! Zabaduk flew in stages. When he got tired he landed on Portia's back. It slowed her down a bit but was less tiring than carrying him – even without his wings. They stopped for lunch at the landfill where the birds rummaged about happily, and timed their arrival for after sunset. While Portia held the cat flap open, Zabaduk said his farewells and climbed back home. He could see just as well in the dark and gazed around him. Only a week or so, he thought, but it seems a lifetime. He curled up on his sofa and went to sleep.

⇒⋐

"Aunt Eliza! Look! Look at Zabaduk, he's changed! He's a *Dragon!*" cried Sammy in excitement.

"Why, so he is. I always thought there was something strange about him – his ears were not right, and his tail was too short. But my, look at him now. How on earth did it happen? Perhaps Giaccomo knows something about it. Why don't we go and see him? Let's take Zabaduk to show him."

"Yes, yes. Let's go now!"

Sammy's parents were equally amazed, but left it to Aunt Eliza, whose present he was, to see the toy seller.

Giaccomo had received a very strange letter in ancient Italian, which took him back to his schooldays. He had to get an old dictionary to understand all of it.

"What a strange story," he marvelled. "How can I possibly explain all this to Eliza? I knew Maladok was no good, but – this beats all. I suppose I will just have to try. I do have Milo's letter."

A few days later he received the expected visit. He picked up Zabaduk and examined him closely.

"My goodness, what a wonderful transformation!' he said. "I knew Milo was good, but – this! You must be very proud, Zabaduk."

Zabaduk looked at him with a happy smile. It was clear enough what Giaccomo was saying. And he *was* proud; proud of himself, proud of all his friends and especially proud of the Great (and skilful) Magician who had given him his new life.

"Isn't he wonderful?" said Aunt Eliza. "If you had shown me the real Zabaduk I should never have afforded him. Do you know how it happened?"

"Well, yes," replied Giaccomo tentatively, "but I am not sure how much you will believe. Why don't you all sit down? It's quite a long story."

So they all sat around, with Zabaduk back on Sammy's lap, and listened to Giaccomo's story. When he had finished he showed Aunt Eliza the letter from Merlin. But although she was a school teacher she could not make much of it.

"What lovely paper," she remarked "and just look at that seal – it's a dragon!"

"Yes, Milo was always fond of dragons," said Giaccomo. "That's why he made such a wonderful job, I suppose. He's an old Celt, you know, though he learned his trade in Italy, long ago. Speaks the most strange language. But I haven't seen him for years, living as he does, like a hermit."

"Can we meet him?" said Sammy excitedly.

"No, no," replied Giaccomo. "He would be most embarrassed. He would not understand you, and might feel that he would be losing some of his power. He only speaks to animals and toys."

"Oh," said Sammy in disappointment. "Well, can I write him a letter?"

"I am sure he would love that," said Giaccomo. "If you leave it with me, I will make sure he gets it."

I am not sure how much Aunt Eliza believed, but Sammy had no doubts. "Maybe one day I will learn how to speak to you," he said fondly to Zabaduk.

≡≡

There was a tap on the window. It was very early in the morning and the sun had not yet risen. Zabaduk unfurled his new wings and flew gracefully on to the sill. He could only fly of course from sunset to sunrise, and never flew unless everyone in the house (except Molly) was safely in bed.

"Hi, Wendy," he greeted her. "Up for the worms? Have you seen anything of Breezy?"

"He comes sometimes," replied the wren, "usually when it's stormy. But he has a new job, you know!"

"I couldn't imagine him spending his life among those gossipy seabirds," said Zabaduk. "What's he doing now?"

"He does Merlin's seamail – or should it be airmail? – anyway overseas. I can't imagine there's a lot, but Merlin does have contacts abroad, especially in Italy, where he gets some materials for his toys. It has got dangerous for pelicans and eagles – nasty people take shots at them, but no one bothers seagulls. His tail feathers are growing quickly. All this exercise, I think."

"I would love to see him again," said Zabaduk wistfully. "We ought to get together sometimes."

"Yes, and I would love another ride. If only it wasn't quite so far to the mountain, we could visit the Great Magician. I don't suppose you could fly that far?"

"I don't think so," replied Zabaduk, regretfully. But I have a feeling we will all meet again sometime. You know, I could give you a ride, if you like. Not so far or so high as with Breezy, but it would be fun."

"Great!" said Wendy. "We'll fly round the garden tonight."

And so they did. It was the beginning of a real companionship for Zabaduk. He met all Wendy's bird friends, especially owls – and frightened off a lot of enemies too, those like stalking cats and creatures that pounced in the dark. He could make himself quite fearsome, even though he could never manage to breathe fire.

One day they did meet the Great Magician again – but that's another story.

11. The Great Escape

SAMMY OPENED HIS EYES TO A GREY, gloomy morning. He looked around feeling very strange and sick. There was a throbbing in his head which felt familiar, and frightening. Where was he? He hardly knew if he was awake or still in his dream. He could still see the face of the Great Magician – that was what the animals and birds called him. He had a long white beard and a wonderful smile. That smile was what Sammy hung on to, rather desperately, as his memory crept back. A heavy weight seemed to settle in his tummy and he felt his tears coming. He turned over and hid his head under the pillow. It was a very grubby pillow and smelled of mice and mildew; and now it grew damp with his tears and breath as he sobbed his heart out, remembering the events of the previous day.

He had been playing in the garden with Zabaduk. They were crawling out of a hideaway built among the trees at the very end. It was a snug little home under the low branches of the old yew tree and they had just finished spreading bracken over the floor. This made a fine bed and helped to keep at least some of the mud off his clothes. Sammy was on his knees with Zabaduk under one arm and was just getting to his feet when suddenly an arm snaked around his waist from behind and he was lifted off the ground. He nearly dropped Zabaduk but clutched him wildly as he was carried away over the fence and along the field to the road. He shouted as loud as he could, but was being joggled so much that it came out as a wobbly noise, and there was no one in sight.

Sammy was bundled into a car standing in the road, still carrying Zabaduk. Sitting on the back seat of the car was a woman wearing a track suit. She had grey hair tied back in a bun and wore round steel-rimmed glasses. Her mouth was shut tight in a thin line which gave her a frightening scowl. And she was holding a syringe with a very nasty looking needle. As Sammy collapsed on the seat the woman grabbed his arm and jabbed it with the syringe. Sammy heard the doors slam and the engine start – and then his head started spinning; he felt it throbbing, and then – nothing.

Zabaduk, squashed against Sammy under the smelly blankets which had been flung over them, was equally baffled. He was very sad for Sammy and would have cried if he could. He did not explore during the night, sensing Sammy's need to feel him close, his only contact with the familiar world. But he did wonder what it was all about. These people, he thought, must want something from Sammy's parents. They could not want Sammy for himself. Clearly they did not love him. And he did not think it anything, this time, to do with himself.

He had himself been kidnapped, by the evil toy maker Maladok, who was trying to find out how the Great Magician, Merlin, managed to talk to toys and animals. Maladok had cut off his wings and, in another adventure, he had met Merlin who had given him new ones. For he was a dragon, and could really fly, although only at night when it was too dark for people to see him.

It grew gradually lighter and Sammy became aware of birdsong, and some other noises he could not identify. He also began to be aware of his hunger. He had had no supper. He wondered if they would bring him breakfast. His crying stopped and he poked his head out and released Zabaduk, who rolled on to the floor. Rolling was quite useful to him. Although he could not roll as well as he had without wings, he tucked them in. It would never do for people to see him walking or flying, but they never seemed to notice his rolling. He rolled onto his feet and looked around.

They were in a small room, unused and dusty, and he had the impression from the birds outside that they were high up, perhaps in a tower. There was a small window, about the level of Sammy's head, he thought. He wondered whether he should try to fly up to the sill, but it was already too light.

He listened hard to try to distinguish the different sounds. All sorts seemed to come to his ears. That must be a blackbird, he thought, and that a robin. So they were still in England, or perhaps France – anyway not somewhere like America, or India, those strange places he had heard people talk about. In the distance he heard a rhythmic rushing sound – could that be waves? Then he heard a different sound, a kind of raucous croak which he knew well: a seagull! His hopes rose sky high. I wonder if that could be Breezy? he thought in excitement. Breezy had been his first contact with the Great Magician. Struggling without a tail he had managed to fly all the way to find him. No, the thought, we must be quite lost. It couldn't be him but, that garrulous bunch, they all know one another. They could find him, I'm sure. I wonder if that window opens. All at once he began to feel excited. I'm a *dragon*, he remembered, and this is a new adventure. He would get them out of this hole. Those silly people, he muttered, they don't realise who they have captured.

While he was thinking, and beginning to plan, the door opened with a loud creak and the woman came in. Sammy sat up and watched as she kicked Zabaduk out of her way and plonked a tray down on the floor. She looked at Sammy and seemed relieved to see him awake.

"Breakfast," she said abruptly, and stomped out before he could ask any questions.

Breakfast proved to be a pot of tea with some milk and sugar, and slices of bread and butter. Sammy looked at it balefully. She can't know much about children, thought Zabaduk. No cornflakes, no egg, no toast, no orange juice, no jam or marmalade.

Sammy got up and stretched. However dull, it was food, he thought, and he was certainly hungry enough. He wandered over to the bathroom and Zabaduk heard water flowing and splashing.

I don't imagine they brought a toothbrush, he thought. Sammy returned and sat on the floor. He poured himself a cup of tea, adding milk and plenty of sugar. Zabaduk surreptitiously rolled on to his feet and watched as Sammy sipped his tea and devoured the bread and butter. It didn't take him very long. He wandered to the window and looked out. And rubbed his eyes.

"Wow, Zabby! we're somewhere by the sea."

"I could have told you," muttered Zabaduk who knew Sammy would not hear. I wonder if he will open the window, he thought.

Sammy gazed out at the scene before him. The room was high up in what seemed to be an old house, though Sammy thought it must have been left empty. The dormer window was closed. Under it was a short stretch of roof ending at a narrow walkway protected on the outside by a low wall. He could not look straight down, but he thought they must be in an attic. In front of him the rough ground sloped downwards to the edge of a cliff. He could see the height of the cliffs by looking to the left where they swept round and out. Flocks of sea birds spiralled around the cliff tops and the rocks below where the waves broke in a rhythmic hiss and crash. It was quite stuffy in the room which smelled of mould and he looked at the window to see if it would open. He drew the bolt at the bottom and tried to lift the latch. It was stiff but he manage to lift it, standing on his toes, so that it remained in an open position. But he could not push the window open. It must have been stuck for years, and warped. Disappointed he looked around the room and saw an old broom leaning against the wall.

"Go on!" shouted Zabaduk, "Bang it open!" If only he could hear me, he thought, not for the first time. But Sammy did not need advice or cheering on. He held the broom with the brush in front like a lance and ran at the window.

Bang! The broom hit the window just by the latch and it burst open. The nearest pane cracked but did not fall out. A gust of wind blew in: clean, fresh air with a smell of salt and seaweed. The noise of the sea was now much louder and the call of the birds seemed friendly. Sammy gave a cheer.

⇒⇐

Aunt Eliza sat in the small sitting room at the back of Giaccomo's toy shop drinking a cup of coffee and chatting to the toy seller. They had become good friends since Zabaduk's last adventure. How surprised everyone had been when the toy "snake" suddenly sprouted wings overnight! Giaccomo knew at once that the repairs had been the work of Merlin, or "Milo" as he knew him. As soon as Aunt Eliza heard about Sammy's kidnap she went to consult him. Sammy's parents, Mr and Mrs Grant, did not want to risk putting Sammy into more danger and had asked her not to tell anybody. But Giaccomo was special, and Aunt Eliza felt that he might understand what was happening and what to do. He was, of course, horrified.

"But I don't think it can be anything to do with Zabaduk," was his immediate thought. "It must surely be something to do with Sammy's parents. They must have something, or else know something, that the kidnappers want."

"Yes," agreed Aunt Eliza, "but isn't it strange, happening so soon after Zabby's adventure? It looks as though there must be some connection."

Giaccomo thought for a while. "I wonder if there's an Italian connection," he said. "I am sure that Maladok must have heard about Zabaduk and be very angry. He might want to take revenge. And I know he has connections with the Mafia in Italy, where he came from long ago." He laughed. "All good – or notorious – toy makers seem to come from Italy, and he is not from Milan like Milo and me – he's from Sicily, the home of the Mafia."

"Do you mean the gangsters?" asked Aunt Eliza, rather horrified.

"Yes, but what could it be that the Mafia might want?" asked Giaccomo. "They wouldn't go kidnapping just to please Maladok. He's only what they call a 'foot soldier' – not a VIP."

This was Aunt Eliza's turn to think.

"Sammy's father is a scientist," she said. "I think I caught some reference to an important invention he has made, but they – Sammy's parents – hushed it up almost immediately. I seem to remember it had to do with making cars run on water instead of petrol. Mr Grant was worried that the oil companies would somehow stop him. Although being so important in protecting the climate it would upset the oil business."

"Yes, and not all oil companies, or their governments, are honest. It would be quite possible for the Mafia to approach one of them with an offer. So long as Sammy is a prisoner Mr. Grant would not dare make his invention known. But it is also possible that the Mafia themselves might wish to steal the invention to sell it or, perhaps, to make Mr. Grant pay a part of everything he earns from it. Whatever the reason, Sammy is the key. We must get him free! You know, I do believe that Milo could find him. He must have the biggest airforce in the world – all his feathered friends!"

"Could you ask him?"

"Well, the difficulty is that I can't reach him directly," replied Giaccomo, "I always have to wait for him to send me one of his messengers." He sighed. "I wish I had a tame bird. I think that next time he sends me something I will ask him if he can persuade one of his pigeons to live with me as a carrier. Perhaps a pair could settle with me. He would have to teach them a signal I could give them, like 'go to Milo'."

"Yes, a lovely idea, but what can we do now?" asked Aunt Eliza.

"I don't think we can do anything from here," replied Giaccomo, "but don't despair. Remember Zabaduk is with Sammy, and I am sure he can talk to the birds."

"Talk to the birds!" exclaimed Aunt Eliza.

"Milo talks to his toys as well as his animals, you know. That was the source of all the trouble with Maladok.

"Yes," he continued, "I am sure that Zabaduk can talk to animals and birds, somehow. Don't ask me how, because I couldn't begin to explain! But that was why Maladok began to cut him up – to find out what was inside; but of course there was nothing to see. It's as if scientists could find out what we think by cutting up our brains. Just as well they never will!

"Anyway I feel sure that Zabaduk will get a message out. We will have to wait as patiently as we can. Sammy will come to no harm while he is still useful to the kidnappers."

"But what about Sammy's parents?" asked Aunt Eliza. "They will never believe Zabby can rescue him."

"No. Scientists make the worst believers! It will be a hard time for them. Worse than for Sammy and Zabaduk. They will be waiting for a message, and won't dare tell the police in the meantime. I think all you can do is to comfort them; try to impress upon them how brave and resourceful Sammy is. I feel that something good will come out of all this trouble. You have always wanted to meet Milo – who knows? Perhaps you will!"

Aunt Eliza cheered up a little. There was something very comforting about the old toy maker.

"Oh, well. I'll do my best," she said, as she left.

≡≡

Zabaduk heard or felt footsteps clumping up the stairs and wondered if Sammy was hearing them too. Then he saw him turn round and quickly but carefully close the window without jamming it.

Thank goodness, thought Zabaduk, I hoped he would. I wonder

if she will notice the cracked pane. But it wasn't the breakfast woman. This time it was a man. He threw open the door and glanced quickly around.

"What that noise?" he asked, glaring at Sammy.

"Fell down," said Sammy, rubbing his knee.

The man continued to glare suspiciously at Sammy. He was dark-skinned, small and rather stout, and looked unshaven. Eventually he pointed his finger.

"You keep quiet!" he said roughly, "No make noise!" "I have stick, yes?"

He turned round and stomped out, locking the door behind him. Sammy sat down on the bed. He was trembling and looked rather pale. Zabaduk longed to comfort him. Don't worry, he wanted to say, he looks all bark, that one. Sammy caught sight of Zabaduk on the floor and picked him up. He went back to the bed and lay down on his front, beginning to cry again and cuddling Zabaduk tight.

"Oh Zabby, what are we to do?" he sobbed.

Zabaduk was relieved to be able to give him some comfort. "I wonder if he heard my thoughts?" he said to himself. "If only I could get him to open the window again and leave some crumbs." He tried hard to suggest this. To his surprise he saw Sammy open his eyes and look at the window.

"Go on! Go on!" shouted Zabaduk. Sammy rolled over on his back but did not get up. But he kept looking at the window.

Perhaps shouting is not the best way, thought the dragon. What was I doing before? He thought hard about all the sights and sounds Sammy must have experienced when he looked out. He could see that Sammy had stopped crying. Lying on the bed, in spite of being crushed, he could see the sky through the window and birds flying across in the distance.

Oh how I wish I was out there flying with them! He thought. Then he felt Sammy sigh and get up. He watched him walk over to the window and open it. They both saw the robin perched on the low wall outside.

Sammy smiled. "Hello robin," he said quietly. "Waiting for crumbs? Let's see what we can find."

He gathered up the crumbs remaining from breakfast, and spread them over the sill. Then he retreated to the bed and the two of them watched.

The robin cocked his head on one side and then the other and chirruped. Then flew over to the window sill and began pecking at the crumbs.

Just like Wendy, thought Zabaduk. I wonder if he will talk to me. Wendy, a wren, had been his first outside friend.

"Hello," he said. "What's your name?" He spoke quite softly, although he knew it was not really necessary. But in all his other conversations with animals and birds Sammy had not been present – usually away at school – and he felt a bit bashful. But the robin heard clearly and looked up in great surprise.

"Hello!" he exclaimed. "What kind of creature are you?"

"I'm a dragon – not a real one" he explained quickly as the robin jumped. "I'm a toy dragon, but I can talk, at least to some people, and I can fly, though not in the day time. I'm called Zabaduk – Zabby to my friends. We – that is my friend Sammy there and I – are in great trouble. Could you help us?"

"Well, maybe. Depends what you need. I'm just called Robin. I don't move about much. This is my garden, my home, but I know just about everyone who comes in. So does my wife, Ruby. Thank your friend for the crumbs. Most obliging."

"It's difficult for me to talk while Sammy is awake. Better at night, but that's not so good for you, is it? Could you come early in the morning, as soon as you wake?"

"OK. See you tomorrow!" And off he flew.

The rest of the day was terribly boring for the two of them, but especially for Sammy who had nothing to do. Shutting up a six-year-old boy, used to going to school, playing with toys and friends and running about in the garden, all day in an empty room, is really very cruel. He spent most of it gazing out of the window, occasionally putting out what crumbs he could find in the hope of attracting more birds, or lying on the bed, cuddling Zabaduk. A lot of tears were shed.

Zabaduk did his best to comfort him, with some success. He felt at times that Sammy was responding to his thoughts and practised hard to think up encouraging pictures. Sometimes Sammy would look hard at him and turn him around so that he could look into his face.

"You know," he said after a long while, "I really do think you are trying to talk to me!"

Zabaduk tried to smile and went as far as cocking his head – just a weenie bit, so that it might have been a movement of Sammy that caused it. He imagined himself flying in circles above the cliff top.

"Oh, Zabby, wouldn't it be wonderful if you really could fly!" sighed Sammy, almost in reply.

"But I can, I can!" shouted Zabaduk, and then realised that this was not the way to talk, and might even lead to trouble. It might be best if Sammy did not know this – for a while at least. But it was wonderful to be able to talk just a little bit. Sammy needed company, and not just an ordinary toy. He felt he was succeeding in raising Sammy's spirits and giving him hope.

At lunch time the woman brought a plate of spaghetti, some more bread and a jug of water. "Good," muttered Zabaduk. "More crumbs. We may need them."

By the evening Zabaduk found that he could attract Sammy's attention by his original image of flying over the cliff. It seemed to be a kind of trigger, that made Sammy pick him up and pay attention to what he was trying to say. He, himself, had no difficulty understanding Sammy, though sometimes he could feel that the words he heard did not exactly fit the thoughts he could also hear!

$$\Longrightarrow\Longleftarrow$$

That night Sammy found it very difficult to sleep. He kept thinking of his home, his beloved Mummy and Daddy and Aunt Eliza. Zabaduk caught images of various memories of happy times, and found himself sharing a lot of Sammy's homesick suffering. He tried as hard as he could to cheer him up with scenes of escape. This was not difficult since his own imagination was full of possible plans. He also tried to send some of his thoughts to Merlin and once seemed to see him clearly in his workshop, talking to Whirlwind, the great eagle who guarded his mountain, though he could not catch what was said. Eventually, nearing midnight, Sammy seemed to relax and soon after fall asleep.

When he was sure that Sammy would not wake, Zabaduk carefully wriggled free from his embrace and looked at the window which, luckily, was still open. It was a clear, slightly chilly night and he could see that the moon was bright. He hopped on to the floor and with a great feeling of relief raised his wings and flew on to the sill. It was a silent world out there in the garden. He heard an owl call and, further away, a fox's bark. He gave a cry "Zabadabadaba!" and launched off the sill. One flap took him to the wall, a bounce, and then off he dived, swooping in ecstasy almost to the ground before he flapped his way up to the chimney pots, around the house and away to the sea.

He flew along the tops of the cliffs, looking at the seagulls sleeping on the waves and the shoreline. Nothing seemed to be stirring. Out at sea he thought he saw movement, rather far off, and turned in curiosity to see a little better. As he flew nearer he made out a patch of white splashes. Dark bodies seemed to leap out of the water, flashing briefly in the moonlight before diving back into the dark sea, throwing up gleaming droplets.

"Goodness," he gasped, "what can they be? Some kind of fish? I wonder if they are dangerous." Realising that they could hardly leap to his height he circled over them and tried calling:

"Heh! You down there, who are you?"

One of the creature twisted in mid air in surprise, falling on his back with a great splash. To his own surprise, Zabaduk heard giggling all around.

"We're dolphins!" they all shrieked," and one voice came "But who on earth are you?"

"I'm Zabaduk. I'm a dragon – not a real one!" he shouted straight away. He was learning fast how the word frightened his animal friends. Most of the dolphins had already dived down deep, but one of them seemed to be more sensible, or braver. He was lying on his back, looking up.

"Silly lot of kids!" he exclaimed. "I knew you couldn't be a real dragon, not grown up at least, but I never knew they could be as small as you. Are you very young?"

"No, I'm a toy, but a very special one. I was made by the Great Magician – do you know him?"

"A toy! Flying and talking?"

"Yes. I can't explain everything now, but we're in big trouble – my friend Sammy and I. He's a little boy and I belong to him. We've been kidnapped and we need to get a message to the Great Magician, – Merlin some call him. Do you know him?"

The dolphin gave a spin.

"Kidnapped! Wow, how exciting! I've heard of Merlin of course, but never seen him. Does he swim?"

This took Zabaduk by surprise. Of course, it was unlikely that Merlin met sea creatures. But anything was possible with him.

"I don't know. He's very old, but he may have when he was younger. He lives not far from the sea, but I have no idea where we are, here."

"Tell you what – my name's Nosy, by the way – I can call up

the old ones – we can call them from a long way off, you know, and see if they can help."

By this time all the other dolphins had recovered from their fright and were swimming in a circle around Nosy and Zabaduk, listening.

"Oh, thank you!" said Zabaduk. "I am getting very tired and its a long way back. I'll come back tomorrow if I can, or later if I can't make it. Will you be around?"

"You bet! Wouldn't miss this adventure for worlds. We'll see what we can find out in the meantime. Bye, bye!"

"Bye, and thanks again," said Zabaduk as he set off back to the coast.

———

True to his word Robin appeared on the open windowsill as soon as it began to grow light and the birds in the garden had started, here and there, their morning songs.

"Hi Zabby! Are you awake? What's this all about?"

"Hello Robin, thanks for coming. We've been kidnapped!"

"Wow! How did it happen, and what do they want?"

"We were grabbed out in the garden, I don't know why. It may be to do with Sammy's parents, I suppose. But we need to escape. You don't happen to know any seagulls?"

"Seagulls! What do you want with them. Noisy lot of yobs! Always quarrelling and bullying each other."

"Well, I have a friend called Breezy. He's a seagull who lost his tail and had it fixed by the Great Magician – Merlin they call him. We need to get a message through to him – the Great Magician I mean. I am sure he will know what to do. I have no idea where we are. I am sure that any seagulls around would know how to get hold of Breezy. He must be quite famous! Breezy will know the way to Merlin's mountain."

Robin pecked at some of the crumbs Sammy had spread on the sill while he thought.

"I don't really have anything to do with seagulls," he said. "Tell the truth, I keep away from them. When they get into one of their tizzies they don't really know who or what they are pecking at. They could chop me in two without even knowing it! What I can do, I can ask my friend Percy. He's a very lazy pigeon, but big enough not to be scared of them. The only difficulty will be to get him off his perch. But he's a friendly bird, and his mate Pickles may help. She's a sweetheart, but right now busy with her brood or I'd ask her." He made up his mind suddenly, as before.

"OK, see you later, thanks for the crumbs!" And off he flew.

Zabaduk wondered what "later" meant, but was greatly heartened. Hooray! he thought, things are beginning to roll. He curled up by Sammy's feet and waited, hoping that Robin might return before Sammy woke. It was still very early. The birdsong was increasing in volume and, with the window open, he thought it might wake Sammy. But Sammy was dead to the world after his difficult night.

Zabaduk let his thoughts wander. Even if the seagulls have heard of Breezy, he thought, they may not know where he is or where to find him. Those seagulls, they don't really like going far from their own patch – unless there's a storm. That may be the best bet. But I don't want to wait for a storm. It may never come. Oh well, no use worrying until there is something real to worry about.

His thoughts were disturbed by a low whistle.

"Zabby!"

"Hello Robin, you are back soon."

"Yes, well, Percy agreed to do what he can, but I had to promise him food! He is greedy as well as lazy. They seem to go together, don't they? Try to get Sammy to put out some bigger bits of bread.

Do you think you could do that? I don't know if you two can talk."

"I'm not sure either. Up to yesterday I would have said we couldn't. But somehow I think we are beginning to learn how to do it. It's certainly not an exact science. I may be able to manage it, or Percy may be disappointed. Will he be cross if he doesn't find much?"

"Oh no; he's too lazy to be cross. On the other hand he may be less inclined to help. Do what you can. He may arrive while I'm away. I told him he would not find much until you had finished breakfast. Well I must be off again, I have young to feed too, you know. Hope you get on all right. Bye, bye!" And off he went again.

Breakfast arrived while Sammy was still asleep. Again it consisted of tea and slices of bread and butter. Sammy rubbed his eyes and looked at it grumpily. Zabaduk took the opportunity to think hard of empty tummies, cornflakes, porridge, eggs and bacon. Since he was never hungry himself this was tricky. However Sammy got the message and called out to the woman:

"Hey! I want a proper breakfast! Porridge or cornflakes, eggs and bacon, toast and marmalade!"

The woman turned and looked at him rather doubtfully.

"You more hungry?" she asked. "I see." She stomped off.

Zabaduk looked at Sammy as best he could and imagined birds and especially pigeons.

"Now what are you trying to tell me?" asked Sammy "What's all this about birds? Pigeons?"

Zabaduk pictured hungry pigeons, nests and fledglings.

"I don't know what this is all about, Zabby, but I'm sure you are trying to tell me something. Have you made some friends? I bet you have, and one of them must be a pigeon. Ok I'll put something out, but let's see what she brings first."

While this conversation was taking place there was a loud

rustle of wings and a very fat pigeon settled on the wall outside the window.

Oh dear, he's too early, thought Zabaduk, but Sammy was amazed. He looked at Zabaduk.

"How did you know?" he asked. Zabaduk thought of the robin. "Oho! You've been talking to the robin. This is beginning to get exciting. You can talk to them too!"

Zabaduk thought about the robin and the pigeon talking, and when he believed that Sammy had understood him, he thought about the pigeon talking to a seagull.

"Wow, this is getting complicated," said Sammy. "Who have you been talking to . A seagull now?"

While this was going on Percy was listening and cocking his head. Now he gave a low warble and spoke to Zabaduk.

"Hello, you must be Zabaduk, I imagine, and the boy must be Sammy? Can he hear me? He seems to have difficulty understanding you."

"Gracious! I really don't know any more. He couldn't understand me until yesterday. Possibly if you think hard about something, or better still keep a picture in your mind of something very important to you, he might pick it up. It seems to be on that kind of wavelength. Have a go!"

Percy looked at Sammy with his head cocked and imagined Pickles sitting on her nest with two hungry little mouths squawking. Sammy was looking at him with a puzzled expression.

"Is he trying to say something, Zabby? I feel sure he is, but I don't really understand what."

Zabaduk, who got the picture quite clearly, imagined it himself and immediately Sammy clapped his hands, startling Percy, who flapped into the air, made a brief circle and landed again with an angry warble.

"Tell your friend not to do that!"

Sammy was immediately contrite. "So sorry, bird. I wonder what your name is. Zabby, tell him I won't do it again. But I think we had better eat something before the woman comes back, if she does. I am hungry anyway. I'll put some crumbs out. Would you warn him?"

As Zabaduk transmitted the message, Sammy got up and broke up some of the bread, spreading the bits over the sill. Percy watched him undisturbed. When Sammy retreated a little he flapped on to the sill and began eating. Sammy began eating too, spreading some bread and pouring himself a cup of tea. Zabaduk wondered how to tell Sammy Percy's name, but gave up. It was all too confusing.

While they were eating – except Zabaduk, the woman came in carrying a plate of scrambled eggs. Percy had retreated to the roof as the door opened, so she did not see him, but did see some of the crumbs.

"You eat all bread!" she said angrily. "Eat all eggs. Tomorrow porridge."

"Do you suppose he likes eggs?" asked Sammy. "Well I'll break up some of the toast and put a bit out to see." He spread some of the egg and bits of sodden toast out on the sill.

Percy, having circled to make sure the woman had gone, flew back to the sill and started pecking.

"Tell Sammy thanks," he said. "This soggy toast is splendid. I'll take some back for the children when I go. Now what's all this about seagulls?"

Zabaduk explained about Breezy and the need to get a message to Merlin.

"Well, I don't actually know any seagulls, but I'll see what I can do. Trouble is, if I get too close while they are eating they will drive me off. Inhospitable lot, they are. I'll have to wait for an opportunity when I find one who has had his fill. I'll come back when I have some news. Thanks again." He filled his beak with the remainder of the soggy toast, gave a muffled warble to Sammy, and flew off back to his nest.

———⫸⫷———

Arriving home, Percy distributed the soggy toast to the two off-spring and consulted his wife about where to find a helpful seagull.

"Goodness, I can't imagine," Pickles replied. "But I'm so bored here with these insatiable creatures, why don't I go and look around? But they need more breakfast too. One lot of toast doesn't go far with them! Keep an eye on them for a bit."

Percy settled on a branch by the nest, quite happy to let Pickles do the scrounging, while she took off towards the coast. She soon spotted a group of seagulls fighting over some small dead fish left on the beach by fishermen where they had dropped through the net. She settled a safe distance away and watched them. One of the older seagulls was clearly getting the best of it. The others seemed to leave him alone. They certainly treated him with unusual respect. He wore the scars of numerous battles. There was a bald patch on his head and many of his feathers were shaggy. One eye, too, looked a bit odd. Having eaten his fill for the time being, the veteran found himself a place out of the wind and settled down for a snooze.

I wonder, thought Pickles. He doesn't look friendly, but I bet he knows a lot. Plucking up her courage she waddled carefully towards him to where she could talk above the noise of the younger ones, still battling away.

"Excuse me, sir," she said politely. "I wonder if you could give me some advice?"

The seagull turned his good eye towards her and gave her a hard look. (Now I understand what is meant by "A beady eye" thought Pickles.) However the seagull seemed to like what he saw.

"And what would a plump young pigeon like you want with an old seadog like me?" he grunted.

Although he sounded grumpy, Pickles could see he was not displeased, he was even amused.

"Do you happen to know a seagull called Breezy?" she asked.

"Breezy, that jumped-up rascal? What can you want with him?"

"Well, he's a friend of a friend of a friend of my husband's," replied Pickles rather doubtfully. "The thing is," she went on quickly, "this last friend is in big trouble, "he and – his young master – have been kidnapped. They need to get a message to the Great Magician, and Breezy is the only one we know who can do it."

" 'Young master', eh", " ruminated the seagull. "And this 'friend' wouldn't happen to be a toy dragon, I don't suppose?"

"Do you know about them?" asked Pickles in great surprise.

"There are rumours flying about all over the place," said the seagull. "I think your Great Magician must have put the word out."

"I wonder how he knew!" remarked Pickles.

"If he's as much of a magician as I've heard," said the seagull, "he'd pick up a distress call from one of his friends, even if he didn't know exactly what was wrong. Well now, if young Breezy has picked up the rumour he'll be flying around looking for you all. Last I heard, he was some way off. I suppose I had better try to put out a word for him. Someone may know where he is."

Suddenly he flapped his wings and gave a huge squawk which made Pickles jump. She saw all the seagulls around stop what they were doing and look at him.

"Anyone know where Breezy is?" he bellowed.

There was a short silence.

"I think he's two coves North, Stroppy," came a timid voice.

"Who's that?" said the seagull, "Titch? Off you go and fetch him. He's wanted urgently. Magician business."

"What, now?" said Titch plaintively. "There's a whole shoal of herring coming in!"

"Yes, now, if you know what's good for you! I'll see some are kept for you."

"OK Stroppy, if that's how it is."

Titch took off, spreading his young wings to catch the breeze, circled once and flew off to the North. Pickles watched it all happening in amazement.

"Wow, Stroppy, you sure have some pull around here!" she exclaimed.

"Should have," replied Stroppy. "They're mostly family. If I'm not their grandfather, I'm certainly their Godfather! He'll be an hour, I daresay. I should go and tell your friends and come back. What's your name, by the way and where have you come from?"

"I'm called Pickles and my lazy husband is Percy. We come from the garden of the old derelict house behind the cliff. The house is where the boy Sammy and his dragon Zabaduk are locked up."

"Hmm, I don't see at the moment how we can get them out. Maybe the magician will magic it somehow. I had better catch some fish for young Titch or he will be upset. See you later!" Off he flew to join his huge family. Pickles could see the fish jumping as they came close to the shore. I wonder what they taste like, she thought. She flew a little closer to the shore and hopped up the beach. One of the seagulls had dropped a bit of fish nearby and she pecked at it tentatively but dropped it in disgust.

"Yuck! I guess I'll leave these to the seagulls," she exclaimed. Just then she saw Stroppy return and settle beside her.

"Don't tell me pigeons have taken to eating fish!" he exclaimed.

"No, just experimenting. Horrible stuff, I can't imagine how you can swallow it."

"Nothing to beat a fresh herring. Well, I came to tell you that things seem to be moving. One of my youngsters has been over to visit the dolphins. It seems that your dragon has been to see them. Gave them quite a shock! Some thought he was a real dragonling. It was night and they couldn't see well. He's supposed to see them again tonight. It occurs to me that it might be a way to get the boy away. Those dolphins are very public-spirited and love playing games. You might suggest it, though that still leaves the difficulty of getting him out of the house."

"How on earth do you mean? Swimming? Surely he would drown?"

"Not a bit. I have seen some dolphins carry quite big boys on their backs, and he's small, isn't he?"

"I think so but I haven't actually seen him," said Pickles. "But if you think it's possible, I'll certainly suggest it."

"I think he would have a lot of fun," said Stroppy. "In fact we could all have a great time. We could give him air support!"

"I think I had better go back and report," said Pickles.

"OK. You will usually find me here, trying to keep the peace. I'll send Breezy over if he gets here, or Titch if he can't be found. Bye, bye."

"Bye, and thanks from all of us."

≡≡≋

Back at the nest Pickles reported everything to Percy. They decided to go to the house together and try to explain everything to Zabaduk, though it might be difficult during the daytime. Soon they were both on the windowsill pecking at the crumbs which Sammy had managed to collect and cooing in an effort to keep his spirits up. Pickles introduced herself to Zabaduk and told her story. Sammy sat on the bed watching the pigeons. He started to get images of seagulls, particularly of one old-timer who seemed to be a chief of some kind, and a younger bird with a rather strange tail. He began to get excited.

"I say, Zabby, are they talking to you?" he said.

Zabaduk was so surprised that he fell over. Since Sammy

was bouncing on the bed he managed to right himself without Sammy really noticing. He gave his trigger image of the cliffs and tried to reinforce some of Pickles' thoughts.

"Wow, I am getting some of it. Keep on doing that!" cried Sammy.

Suddenly he saw a vivid picture of dolphins.

"Dolphins!" he cried. "Are there dolphins here?"

Pickles was explaining what Stroppy had suggested about boys riding on dolphins. Sammy gave a shriek.

"Zabby! are they saying that I could ride on one of them?" Zabaduk, who had never seen a boy on a dolphin did his best to show a picture of what he thought it might be like.

"Zabby we can escape on them! That is, if they are really willing. I remember a story about it. But could I still carry you? I might need both hands to hold on."

This put Zabaduk into a quandary. Should he tell Sammy that he could fly? He spent a long time thinking about this. Merlin had warned him that it could lead to terrible difficulties if he was seen by people, and had even let him believe that he would only

be able to fly at night. But he had never been sure how far the warning extended to Sammy, and this was clearly an emergency. He felt that if he ever really had to he could manage to fly with Sammy. But although he could fly, he could not do it for long distances. When returning from Merlin's mountain last winter he had grown tired quite often and had to have rests on Portia's back.

Portia was a pelican who carried parcels – and sometimes even small creatures – for Merlin. Also he was not at all sure what would happen if he got wet, which he almost certainly would, flying over the dolphins. They were not exactly a restful bunch. As far as he knew, real dragons loved swimming, but he was only a toy. He thought about trying to fly with heavy wet wings, and groaned. The only way round the problem, he decided, was to persuade the dolphins to keep close to the shore so that he could go in and rest when he needed to.

He spent so long thinking that Sammy was puzzled, and a little worried, by Zabaduk's apparent silence. Their 'conversations' were so new that he thought maybe he had been imagining them.

"Zabby!" he cried. "Are you still there?"

Brought back to earth, Zabby tried to reassure him by sending out his trigger image. Suddenly he decided that there was no way they were going to escape without Sammy knowing that he could move and fly. After all, it was difficult enough for Sammy to learn to read Zabby's thoughts and he was learning that fast!

Taking his own equivalent of a deep breath he turned his head and looked at Sammy and gave as sharp a picture as he could of the dolphins swimming and a dragon flying above them.

"Oh Zabby," sighed Sammy. "If only you could!"

Zabaduk saw that Sammy had not realised that he had moved his head. He turned away slowly and walked deliberately round the room.

Sammy watched in amazement, his hand over his mouth as

his dragon finally returned to the middle of the room and looked at him. Then Zabaduk looked towards the window, took another of his imaginary breaths and launched himself into the air – and out into the garden!

Percy and Pickles had just time to scuttle out of the way, scattering crumbs. Sammy rushed over to look out and saw Zabaduk and his two friends circling over the trees, Zabaduk playfully chasing them and trying to grab their tails. Eventually they all returned to the window, the two pigeons settling on the wall and Zabaduk on the sill.

"Zabby! Oh Zabby, you're a real dragon!" cried Sammy. Why did you never tell me?"

Zabaduk tried to send a picture of Merlin pointing his finger at him, and then of all the grown-up people around Sammy.

"I think I see," said Sammy. "Merlin must have warned you it would lead to trouble. Well, I am certainly glad you showed me. Now we must be able to escape! But how am I going to get out of this room? I wish I could fly too."

Zabaduk sent him another picture of Merlin, and one of Breezy.

"Is that your seagull friend? Will I see him?"

Zabaduk nodded his head, and Sammy clapped his hands, disturbing Percy and Pickles again.

"Oh, sorry birds!" he exclaimed as the birds settled once more.

"That was a lot of fun," said Percy, but we must be off now to feed our brood. They will be ravenous. Breezy should be here before too long. One of us will keep an eye open for him at the beach. Bye, bye." And the pigeons flew off. Zabaduk tried to explain with a picture of the nest and the fledglings. He flew down to the floor again and was just in time, as the door opened and the woman came in with lunch – fish pie, mashed potatoes and peas.

"Yuck!" said Sammy who did not care much for fish. But Zabaduk gave him a picture of a happy seagull on the windowsill.

"Oh well," sighed Sammy, "Everything seems to be getting rather fishy, I had better have a go, and your seagull can have the rest." Zabaduk nodded. Really, this is much easier, he thought, now I can nod and shake my head.

Once Sammy had started on the fish pie he found it much better than he had imagined. All the excitement of the morning had given him an appetite, and Percy had eaten too much of his breakfast. But he left some of the pie and put the plate on the windowsill for Breezy although, of course, he couldn't know any of the birds' names. Translating these into images had proved too much for Zabaduk. Then the two friends lay on the bed, waiting. Sammy cuddled Zabaduk and chatted to him happily, and the dragon responded with pictures of the dolphins leaping in and out of the sea, one of them carrying Sammy astride his back, and he himself circling overhead and winging his way to the shore for a rest every so often.

⇒⊱⇐

Titch took nearly an hour to find the flock of seagulls where he believed Breezy was to be found. I'll have to ask around, he thought, and settled near an older bird who looked like the local chief.

"Hello," said the oldie, "haven't seen you before. Come to join us?"

"Well, not exactly, I'm with Stroppy's lot down South. He sent me up to see if I could find Breezy. Is he here?"

"That cheeky rascal. Why does Stroppy want him? Anything to do with all these rumours flying about?"

"Well yes, probably, though I am not sure exactly what it's all about. He's needed to take a message to the Great Magician. As far as we know, he's the only one who knows where to find him."

"If I know Breezy, he'll be delighted. Can't say enough about that magician. I must have heard his tale a hundred times – sorry, no pun intended! – you know the magician gave him a new tail? Anyway there's Breezy, over by that rock."

"Thanks." Titch flew over.

"Are you Breezy?" he asked, settling nearby.

"That's what they call me," replied the bird. "Who are you? I don't remember seeing you before."

"I'm called Titch, though it's a bit much now. I used to be rather small, but I suppose the name will stick! I'm with Stroppy's group further South. He sent me up to find you. It seems you're the only one we know who knows where the Great Magician lives. We've been asked to get a message to him, urgently."

"Oh. I've heard some strange rumours. Is it anything to do with a toy dragon?"

"I think it is, but I am afraid I wasn't told any details. I seem to be Stroppy's messenger these days! Can you come with me? Then maybe we'll manage to find out what it's all about."

"I wouldn't mind an excuse to see Merlin again," said Breezy. "Come on, let's go. Lead on!"

The seagulls lost no time flying back to Stroppy who filled them in as best he could with Pickles' story and told Breezy where to go to find Zabaduk and Sammy. Titch felt he deserved to go too, having done all the hard work finding Breezy. The seagulls landed on the wall and Breezy gave one of his huge squawks. But the two friends needed no call – they had been watching with increasing impatience

"Breezy!" cried Zabaduk. "Hooray! Just the fellow we need. Did Titch find you all right? I suppose he must have done, silly question. Have you had our story explained?"

"Not all of it, I think. I know you have been kidnapped. How is Sammy coping? He must be in a frightful stew. Are they treating you well?"

"You know, Breezy, it's been an extraordinary experience for us – we've begun to talk! – at least, I have always been able to understand Sammy, but I can get him to understand me a lot of the time, by sending him pictures. I suppose that's really what we do, only much quicker. I am not sure how much he can make out of what you birds say, but I think he picks up some, and I find I can relay it sometimes when he can't. Try saying 'Hello'."

Breezy cocked his head at Sammy and gave one of his bows, which he had learned while staying with Merlin. He gave what he felt was a polite squawk, though it came out almost as a whistle.

"Is he saying hello?" asked Sammy. "Hello seagull, I wish I knew your name!"

Breezy imagined leaves swirling around in the wind. Zabaduk caught the image and imagined it too.

"Wow," said Sammy, "blowing leaves. What can that mean? Are you called 'Windy'?" he asked, looking at Zabaduk.

Zabaduk shook his head and bounced encouragingly.

"Not 'Windy'. Hmm, what about 'Breezy' "?

Breezy and Titch bounced up and down and Zabaduk nodded vigorously.

"Breezy!" shouted Sammy and clapped his hands. The seagulls raised their wings a little but were much less nervous than the pigeons.

"Sorry," said Sammy. "but it's so wonderful to know your name. And who's your friend?"

The others all thought of different ways of picturing small things. The seagulls thought of small birds, and Zabaduk of a miniature dragon.

"Goodness, what can it be," said Sammy. "Something small? – are you called Small?". He looked at Zabaduk for help. Zabaduk shook his head and in some desperation started scratching himself.

"Scratchy? – no. Itchy? – no. I know, it must be Titch!" Zabaduk nodded vigorously and the seagulls hopped up and down.

"Goodness, it's just like charades! But can you help us?"

This was a bit tricky. Breezy squawked and bowed and Zabaduk imagined an open story book with a picture of the Great Magician. Then to give time to tell the whole story to Breezy he told the seagull to start eating the food Sammy had laid out – what Titch had left. Having felt a bit out of it he had used the opportunity to start on the fish pie. Sammy watched the birds making short work of the remains of the pie and tried to follow Zabaduk as he told them the whole story of the kidnap, and the possibility of escaping with the dolphins, if they could somehow get out of the house.

"Of course I will go to Merlin," said Breezy finally. "Luckily I'm still a bachelor. The girls still don't trust my new tail! I hope I can find the way. I last went there from quite a different place – your home. But I know the way there – it's where the wind blows us from the stormy Southwest. If Merlin can't find a way of getting you out, nobody can." Noticing that this seemed to depress his audience, he went on quickly: "If he can give me a tail and Zabby wings, this should be easy for him. And escaping on the dolphins is a brilliant idea. It should be great fun. I'll go and get myself some fresh fish" (he glared at Titch) "and be on my way."

This was too much for Titch. "Please, can I come with you?" he asked earnestly. "I'm still a bachelor too, and I would so love to see the Great Magician; you might need some help. You might even need Stroppy's help, sometime, and I could be a messenger – it seems to be my main job at the moment!"

"Poor old Titch. I certainly don't mind. I could do with some company, but we had better ask Stroppy so that he knows where you are. There may be some fish left there. Come on. Bye, bye you two," he said to Sammy and Zabaduk.

"Wait!" cried Zabaduk, catching Sammy's homesickness just in time to prevent them flying off. "If you are going near Sammy's house, could you take some kind of message?"

"Oh, you clever dragon!" said Sammy, catching a picture of his Mum and Dad reading a letter. "Do let's try to send something. But I have no paper and nothing to write with!"

"Breezy," called Zabaduk. "Do you think you could find some paper and a pencil?"

"No problem," said Titch quickly. "That's my job. I think I know exactly where to go!" He flew off before anyone could answer. While they waited for his return, Sammy thought about what he could write. He knew he couldn't tell them everything. What would they think about the dolphins? They would not believe him, and probably think him crazy with unhappiness. In the end he decided to say simply that he was well, and reasonably treated, and that he still had Zabaduk who was a great comfort. If the message got to Aunt Eliza, she would understand that he had hopes of escape.

Titch returned quicker that they had expected, clutching a piece of paper.

"Sorry, dropped the writing thing. I don't think it's a pencil, but I hope it will work." And he was off again.

Sammy looked at the paper and recognised it as a bill of some kind. Although it was covered with writing he thought he could write over the top. Then Titch was back with a blue object which turned out to be a broken ball point. Sammy tried scribbling on the paper and eventually it produced some quite strong black markings.

"Hooray! It works," he cried. "Brilliant, Titch." He crouched down on the floor and wrote his message out in his large letters.

When Sammy had finished, he was in tears and two drops had fallen on to the paper, smudging the ink a bit. He sniffed and thought about how to tie on the message. But Titch flew on to the floor and dropped an elastic band at Sammy's feet. Sammy looked at him in amazement.

"What a clever bird you are!" he said, smiling down.

Titch preened his wings.

"Tell him to tie the message on my leg, Zabby. I'm the messenger."

But Sammy had already realised this and, having folded the paper, he rolled it around Titch's leg and held it in place with the elastic, being careful to make it firm but not too tight.

Then the seagulls were off in a flurry of wings, the boy and his dragon waving goodbye with sadness to see them go but renewed hope in their hearts.

The room seemed suddenly very empty with the departure of the noisy seagulls, but as they stood looking out into the garden the robin flew on to the windowsill.

"What a lot of visitors you seem to have!" He exclaimed. "No crumbs for a poor robin. What's this muck?" (The seagulls had left a scrappy mess.)

"Fish pie," said Zabaduk. "Not to your taste?"

"Pretty nasty," said Robin, pecking at a bit of potato. "Did you get what you needed?"

"Thanks to you we are full of hope," said Zabaduk. "We really can't thank you enough. Percy and Pickles were a great help too. Breezy (the big seagull) is off with his young friend Titch to find the Great Magician to tell him of our plight. We may be able to escape with the help of the dolphins!"

"Wow, that should be quite an experience. Pity it's a bit too far for me to see it happening. How is Sammy going to get out?"

"We don't know yet," said Zabaduk a bit gloomily. "We hope the Great Magician will help us. Please come whenever you can. We'll do our best to put out crumbs for you. And tell the pigeons not to desert us. We need all the friends we can get."

"Cheer up. I'll come again, and get Percy and Pickles to come too. We all need food, too, with these hungry mouths to feed."

After reporting to Stroppy and having a final feed on some remaining herrings, Breezy and Titch set off to Sammy's home.

"We may get some news from Wendy of what's happening there," explained Breezy. "Wendy is a brave little wren who came with Zabby and me to visit the Great Magician." We can probably leave the message in her care.

Although there was no storm, there was a strong sou'westerly breeze and the birds arrived over Sammy's house towards the evening. They perched on the sitting room windowsill and peered in. It was empty except for the cat, Molly, curled up on the sofa. When Breezy gave a squawk she looked up.

"Hi Breezy! What are you doing here? Have you seen Sammy or Zabaduk? Did they send you?" Lazy as she was, she uncurled and perched on the back of the sofa in a fair degree of excitement.

"Yes. They have been kidnapped – did you know? They are trapped in a house near the sea. We are on our way to the Great Magician to see if he can help them escape. Has anything been happening here?"

"Well, Sammy's Mum and Dad are very unhappy of course. They don't really know what to do. They had a letter which upset them a lot and there was a long conference with Aunt Eliza. They seemed to cheer up a bit after that. I think Aunt Eliza must have told them to trust Sammy. She may even have hinted something about 'friends in high places' – she's a friend of Giaccomo, Merlin's friend. But no police have been here, which I had expected after the last trouble with the burglary. I think the letter must have been a warning."

"Well, we've brought a message from Sammy which we hope will do something to cheer them up. It's tied to Titch's leg – sorry, this young bird is my friend Titch. Titch, meet Molly." Titch tried to emulate Breezy's bow, and failed, nearly falling over. Molly simply smiled.

"Titch was responsible for finding the paper and pen," said

Breezy. He has a brain tucked up somewhere in there. Now we have the problem of getting the message off!" Breezy went on. "Come closer, Titch, let's see what I can do."

"Oh no you don't," said Titch. "I am not trusting that hefty beak of yours! I'll manage myself, thank you." He bent over and attacked the elastic carefully with his own beak. After a lot of fruitless stretching of the band it finally broke, hitting him in the eye.

"Ouch!" he squawked as the message fell off his leg on to the windowsill. "What now? Where should we put it?"

There was a flurry of tiny wings and to Titch's surprise a little wren descended next to him.

"I wondered if all this noise was you, Breezy. Who's your friend?"

"Wendy!" exclaimed Breezy. "How splendid to see you. Have you heard the news too?"

"I know that Sammy and Zabaduk have disappeared, but I suspect you know a lot more," replied Wendy. "What's your story?"

While Wendy was brought up to date, Molly wandered about the room, thinking about where to put the message where it would be noticed immediately and not lost or thrown away. She could see that it was a small scrap of paper, looking too much like a piece of rubbish – which, of course, it was. We need to move things around a bit, she decided. There was a coffee table in front of the sofa with a small lamp on it and also a newspaper and a magazine. She climbed on to the table and with some brisk pawing pushed the newspaper and magazine on to the carpet in a messy heap. Then, as carefully as she could, she upset the lamp so that it lay on its side on the table.

"Wendy!" she called when there was a pause in the conversation. "Could you bring the message here, carefully?"

"That's a good idea," said Wendy, looking at the table and the mess on the floor. She picked up the paper in her beak and flew in, depositing it on the table near the lamp. "Better roll the lamp over the edge of it," she suggested. "They will be sure to see it when they turn the lamp over." Molly managed this with her paw and they looked proudly at their handiwork.

"Great!" said Breezy. "We'll come back here on our way home and you can tell us what happened. We'd better be off and see if we can make the farm by nightfall. It will be late, but the summer evenings are long, now. Not like last winter; do you remember the snow?"

Titch looked almost sad to lose his precious message, but Wendy was so full of praise for his cleverness that he hopped happily from one foot to the other. Then the friends said their farewells and the seagulls flew off into the evening sky.

⇛⇚

Sammy's Mum and Dad were indeed surprised to see the mess in the sitting room when they returned with Aunt Eliza from a visit to their solicitor whom, since they could not seek help from the police, they had decided to bring into their confidence.

Aunt Eliza had pondered long and rather desperately whether to introduce them to Giaccomo, but decided finally that they would simply think her mad. (They already thought her rather strange, but in the nicest way.) The solicitor, an elderly man whose name was Arthur, also happened to be an old friend of Aunt Eliza and had helped Giaccomo in the past when he had arrived from Italy as a refugee. When he learned that Sammy was with a toy dragon from the old toy seller, he was pleasantly surprised and did his best to encourage them.

"Giaccomo's toys are wonderful, you know. Some of them seem to be quite magical. If Sammy has Zabaduk with him he will not feel all alone. Its the best thing I have heard so far." He looked at Aunt Eliza who smiled at him and nodded. But there was little active help he felt able to give.

THE CHRONICLES OF ZABADUK

"Just try to be patient," he said. "The kidnappers, assuming they have Sammy, are sure to make contact soon, and then we can decide on the best thing to do."

Aunt Eliza knew as soon as she saw the state of the room that the disorder was not quite what it seemed. She was the first to move to the table and pick up the lamp.

"Look!" she exclaimed, there's a piece of paper underneath – and something is written on it, some kind of message."

Mr Grant ran over and took the paper from Aunt Eliza.

"Its an old bill – but you're right. Goodness, that must be Sammy's writing!" He read out the message:

I AM FINE. HOUSE IS NEAR SEA. PLENTY TO EAT. STILL HAVE ZABBY WHO IS GREAT. DONT WORRY. SAMMY.

"How wonderful! How on earth did it get here?"

Aunt Eliza just managed to stop herself chuckling. Molly, who had watched the drama from the sofa, jumped down and rubbed herself against her leg.

"Yes, I bet you know how it got here," she murmured under her breath. Aloud she said "Something tells me we are unlikely to find out. But it's so splendid to know that Sammy is well and, seemingly, in good cheer. You know," she went on, "It would not surprise me if he managed to escape. Anyway, you won't need to worry so much while we wait for further news."

Mum and Dad looked at her in amazement.

"Escape!" said Mr Grant. "How on earth? And even if he managed it, how could he possibly get home? It would be more worrying than ever." He looked again at the message.

"Wait a minute," he said. "I wonder if this bill gives us any clues about where he is. Yes, it does say something, but I don't recognise the place. It seems to be in Welsh! Must be some small town or village on the Welsh coast, judging by Sammy's mention of the sea. But what are we to do. We still dare not go to the police. But we had better give the information to Arthur. I believe he knows Wales quite well – or is it Cornwall? I know he jokes about being related to King Arthur. Perhaps he has a solicitor friend nearby who might tell us more."

"Would you like me to take it to him?" asked Aunt Eliza. "I know you would like to be here in case the phone rings."

A little reluctantly, Mr Grant gave her the precious message. It was the only contact he had with Sammy.

"It might be best," he said. I don't want to miss any telephone call."

So Aunt Eliza took the message to Arthur, having first had a good look at it and memorised the name of the shop where the bill had come from. Arthur did not recognise the village but said he would make some careful enquiries. Before going home, Aunt Eliza called on Giaccomo and gave him all the news.

"Well, now there are two possible ways to rescue Sammy," he said. "But I would still put my faith in Merlin to get him out. I just hope the solicitors do not somehow accidentally warn the kidnappers, so that they move Sammy. It's difficult to find lost children without making a big fuss."

"I am sure they will be as careful as they can," said Aunt Eliza, but without help from the police I can't imagine how they will get him out." She returned home thoughtfully.

⇒≡⇐

As the sunset was just lightening the sky Breezy and Titch arrived finally at the farm where Breezy had met Wolly the owl on his first journey to Merlin's mountain. The evening star was clearly visible above the red horizon. It had not been an easy flight. When Breezy had first made the journey it had been winter and now the ground, and the mountain too, looked very different. It was difficult to see in the sunset haze and sometimes hidden by clouds. He had been flying in a kind of corkscrew motion too, and they were now flying much faster. When they got lost Breezy tried flying in the old way to see if the land looked any different. Sometimes this worked when he saw an upside-down river or wood which looked right. That way he also found the rubbish heap where he had rested.

They flew straight into the barn, which was quite dark and alighted on the floor, peering around.

"Hi, Wolly, are you there?" called Breezy.

There was a kind of shuffle above them. "Who's that?" came a deep voice. "Not Breezy is it? I know the voice, but the bird I know flies in circles."

"Of course it's me! Who else could it be? I have a new tail now. At least, it's still growing, but I can fly straight now. The Great Magician worked wonders on it. We are on an urgent mission to see him. Did I ever tell you about Zabaduk? He's a toy dragon made by the Great Magician and who can talk and fly. Anyway he and his friend Sammy – a six-year-old boy– have been kidnapped. We are hoping the Magician can help to find and rescue him."

"What a strange story," said Wolly. "Well, if you managed to see him last time, I expect he will help. Especially as he made Zabaduk. Who's your friend?"

"Oh, sorry, this is young Titch. He found me with a message from Zabby, and has decided to come too."

"Well, find yourselves a nice perch. You know where the compost heap is if you're peckish. I must be off to get food for the family. That means mice for us. No rest for the weary!" He swooped out of the barn with a "Wooh!" of goodbye.

Breezy and Titch made their way over to the compost heap. There was still just enough light for them to rummage about for scraps. Having had their fill they retired to perch on one of the beams and were soon asleep.

Next morning at sunrise they said their good-byes to a very sleepy Wolly and his mate Olive, who had emerged from her

THE CHRONICLES OF ZABADUK

nest and fluffy family, and took off with the mountain now much nearer and clearly visible. They soon saw the wheeling speck that was Whirlwind keeping guard over Merlin's hideaway. The great eagle saw them from a distance and came gliding over to inspect them. Breezy cheekily did one of his corkscrews to introduce himself.

"Well, well, if it isn't young Breezy! I have a feeling that you are expected. There are all kinds of rumours flying around and Merlin keeps mumbling into his beard. Is Zabby in some kind of trouble?"

"Yes indeed!" said Breezy. He has been kidnapped with his friend Sammy. We are all hoping that Merlin can help them to escape. Its quite a story. Perhaps we had better go down, if you will allow us?"

"Follow me!" said the great bird and glided around the peak and down to the shelf in front of Merlin's home with the two seagulls keeping a discreet distance behind. As they settled outside Merlin's home the magician himself emerged, rubbing his hands.

"Splendid, splendid," he cried, "Now perhaps we will get to the truth behind all these rumours! Hello again, Breezy. Who is your young friend? Titch? How do you do, Titch. So nice to meet another friend of Breezy's. You had better all come in and tell your story."

Inside, Breezy told Merlin the story of Sammy and Zabaduk's kidnap, or as much as he knew from the conversation at Sammy's window. He mentioned that the dolphins had offered to carry Sammy away, but that they could think of no way to get Sammy out of the house. Also Breezy was not so confident of Sammy's ability to ride a dolphin as were the dolphins and Sammy himself.

"Well, well, how exciting!" said Merlin at the end of Breezy's recital. It's wonderful to see that Zabaduk is putting his new abilities to such good use. I had great hopes of that young toy."

"Yes, and you know he is beginning to talk to Sammy! Or should I say that Sammy has found a way to understand Zabby? Not all the time, and not so clearly as we can, but he can even understand me sometimes, especially if Zabby helps. He manages to think up clear pictures of what I, and some other birds, are saying. They have made a lot of friends where they are. A robin and a pair of pigeons have been very helpful in finding me – not forgetting Titch, too."

Merlin was very interested. "I wondered if they would manage it. The two of them must be very fond of each other. Its not only pictures, you know, but the feelings that belong to them. Much more difficult for humans, but so much easier for children than grown-ups. Good. Well now, how to get them out? Let's see, Sammy must be six by now. I wonder if Whirlwind could still lift him. What do you think, old friend? Still got enough strength in those dorsals?" Whirlwind gave a mutter of disgust and shook out his huge wings.

"I can still lift a sheep, if I have to!"

"Hmm, not too often I hope. You'll get me into trouble. Stick to rabbits! I wonder – do you think your good wife would help?"

"I know she would be delighted! She's always complaining that I get all the fun."

"Good. But there is one big snag no one seems to have thought of. A six-year-old boy like Sammy couldn't swim all the way here, even supported by dolphins. It's much too cold. He would freeze to death, or catch pneumonia, which is a very dangerous disease."

"Please," said Titch timidly, "I have seen many humans swimming wearing strange suits. I think it is to keep warm. Could not Sammy wear one? ... In fact I saw some people using them down by your harbour as we arrived."

"A special suit, eh! Now why didn't I think of that. What a splendid bird you are, Titch. I wonder what they are like. Probably made of new materials. I can't keep up with science, these days. Probably just as well, I might get in all sorts of trouble. What to do?" Merlin looked at Titch with a twinkle. "Do you think we might borrow one – just to inspect it?"

Titch looked doubtful. "The grown-up size is much too big for me and Breezy to carry. And it would have to be dry. They look very heavy when wet."

"Well, I would dearly love to see one. Might even wear one myself, who knows? I would love to swim with the dolphins. I'm really quite jealous of Sammy!" He thought some more.

"We haven't very much time. You and Breezy go and have a look to see if there is one lying around, and rush back and tell me. I am sure Whirlwind would oblige?"

The eagle bowed and flapped his wings.

Breezy and Titch didn't wait but flew off in a hurry. They glided down the slope of the mountain and winged their way towards the sea, visible in the distance. A stream flowed down the mountain some way to the right of Merlin's home, gradually getting bigger and wider as it collected water from other streams. At the foot it slowed as it reached out over the plain and broadened into an estuary which ended in a small harbour where fishing boats were gathered, some moored to a jetty and some tipped on their sides in the mud and sand of the shore where the tide was low.

"There! Look!" cried Titch.

There was a small wetsuit draped in the sun over the jetty wall.

"Probably a boy's. It looks and feels dry!" he cried excitedly. They hurried back to tell Merlin, who rubbed his hands, delightedly. "Off you go then, Whirlwind."

Whirlwind hopped to the edge of the plateau calling: "Come on you two, show me!"

Soon the birds were all back again, Whirlwind with a small suit in his talons. Merlin examined it closely.

"Yes, some new kind of foam. Nothing I could make. It must hold the water and the body's heat must warm it up. I wonder," he said holding it up. "Hmm. Might be rather big. But the only alternative is to get Giaccomo to buy one. And that might lead to all kinds of complications. I think the poor child will have to do without for a bit. Or, maybe get another. Perhaps we could buy it!"

Merlin went back into the far corner of his cave and came back holding an old leather bag. He shook out a couple of gold coins.

"Well, I don't know what the value of these are nowadays, but I'm sure they would buy a new suit for him," he said.

He found some paper and a pen and wrote carefully:

I HAVE GREAT NEED OF YOUR SUIT FOR AN EMERGENCY. I HOPE THESE COINS WILL BE ACCEPTABLE IN PAYMENT.

He signed with a flourish:

– ORLANDO DI MILANO – and placed the note with the coins in a small cloth bag.

"Now. How to get this to the right person? Breezy, I rely on you and Titch. I don't think it's too heavy for you. Take it down to the jetty and look for a little boy who has lost something. He will probably be crying. When you find him, make sure he finds the bag!"

So the two seagulls flew off again. The bag was heavier than Breezy thought and he staggered finally on to the end of the jetty to rest, while Titch did some exploring. He soon saw the boy, a year or so older than Sammy, he thought, but he was clearly in distress, running backwards and forwards along the jetty and crying. Titch called out to Breezy who came flying over and dropped the bag at the feet of the boy, who stopped crying and looked up in amazement. The birds settled on the jetty some distance off and watched as the boy picked up the bag and opened it, gazing in wonder at the two gold coins. Then he ran off calling: "Mummy, Daddy, look what I've found! A seagull dropped it just by me!"

The birds didn't wait any longer but flew back to tell Merlin what had happened.

"Splendid!" said Merlin when he had heard everything. I think this will do for Sammy. It's quite stretchy and should fit him well enough. What we'll do is this. What we need is a long piece of rope. Who can find me one?"

Titch bounced up and down.

"I can, please! I am the messenger. And I think I can find one if there are any boats around here."

"Thank you again, Titch. But aren't you rather tired? What I need is pretty big and quite heavy. I think you had better take Breezy with you. Then you can each hold one end in your beaks. You are not eagles, you know. Off you go and see what you can find. It needs to be strong enough to lift Sammy and as long as from here to the edge of the cave, or a bit more."

The two seagulls flew off and Merlin explained his plan to Whirlwind.

When the seagulls arrived at the jetty they found a number of seagulls flying around pecking at bits of fish, bait and other left rubbish left on and around the jetty. They called a greeting to the newcomers who settled beside a group sunning themselves on a wall which ran along one side.

"Where have you come from?" asked the local old-timer. "Not from around here, are you?"

"Hi!," said Breezy. "I'm Breezy and this is Titch. We live quite a way round the coast. We are on an errand from the Great Magician. Friends of his (and ours) have been kidnapped and we are planning a rescue."

"Goodness, gracious, how exciting! Tell us all about it."

So the two friends once again went through their story, which was getting just a bit more embroidered each time it was told. Finally they came to the purpose of their visit.

"Have you seen a longish bit of rope lying around anywhere? Something not too heavy but strong enough to hold up a child? I think Merlin figures on using it to lower Sammy out of the window."

The seagulls chattered among themselves for a bit and then one of the younger ones said he thought he knew a piece which might do. A group of them set off with Breezy and Titch along the shore to a clump of rocks where an anchor could be seen in the shallow water stuck between two rocks and attached to a piece of rope which had been cut off to free the boat. Breezy thought the length about right, but how were they to get it free of the anchor?

"Let's try to peck it off, strand by strand," said the old-timer who knew a thing or two. "Here goes!" He began to peck with his strong beak at a bend in the rope where it joined the anchor. He soon broke through two or three strands and then made way for another bird, and they all took turns. In a surprisingly short time the rope was free.

"Great!" said Breezy. "Thanks so much. You have all been terrific. Now Titch and I must try to lift it by the ends."

But the rope turned out to be longer and heavier than they had realised. The two friends could barely raise it off the ground and found themselves almost colliding as its weight pulled them together.

"Hang on!" cried the old-timer, "We'll all help. I'll take the middle. You, Croaky go a bit to the left and Creaky, you go to my right!"

The result was a strange sight. The five seagulls spread themselves out in a line and then managed to fly up with the rope held in their beaks. But they could not open their beaks to speak!

We had better fly straight there, thought Breezy. He gave a tug at his end and started to fly off towards the mountain. The others understood what he was trying to do and turned to fly with him. So the wavy line of seagulls flew along the river until they grew so tired they had to rest. The old-timer in the middle (his name was Poky) grew tired first and simply flew down, pulling them all down with him until they landed gasping on the river bank. After a rest Breezy picked up his end of the rope and at his signal they resumed their course. They needed two more rests before they finally flopped on to Merlin's shelf, quite worn out.

"Well done, well done," cried Merlin as they dropped the rope. "A splendid achievement! And how nice to make some new friends. Would you tell me your names?

The birds looked amazed at being spoken to by a human, but politely called out their names. Then they all sat in a row on the edge of the plateau to see what would happen next.

Merlin inspected the rope. "It looks awfully heavy. We must try to lighten it." He spread it in a straight line along the shelf and they could see that it was indeed longer than seemed necessary, so he fetched a knife and cut off about a third.

"That should do the trick," he said. "Whirlwind and Gale are much stronger and can lift much more easily with their claws, and breathe properly!" Whirlwind's mate Gale was perched next to him.

The birds all gathered round Merlin while he explained what he had in mind.

"Whirlwind and Gale must keep out of sight on the roof or a nearby tree. There are nasty people around who would love to shoot them, and we don't want to frighten Sammy until things are explained. They can drop the rope below the window, but not until it's dark enough for it not to be noticed. It would probably be best for the escape to take place at first light, which is early enough now for everyone to be asleep. Breezy must explain everything to Zabaduk who can now, hopefully, translate it all to Sammy. Breezy and Titch together will then lift the middle of the rope and pass it through the window to Sammy, who needs to take a loop around his chest, under his shoulders, and hold tight to the rope on each side. Then, while he stands in the gutter behind the wall, Whirlwind and Gale will have to take an end of the rope each and lift Sammy carefully. If all goes well they can carry him clear of the wall and lower him to the ground. Do you all understand what you have to do?"

This seemed clear enough and they all gave noises of agreement.

"What about us?" said one of the local seagulls. "Can't we help too?"

Merlin considered. "I think it would be splendid if you all went, if you want to. We don't know that everything will go according to plan; there might be an emergency. You may want to get a message to me. Also, I have a feeling that Maladok has something to do with the kidnap and may interfere. You may find a hawk or two buzzing about, or even other creatures. There is safety in numbers."

"What about the wetsuit?" asked Breezy.

"Good for you! It might be best for Whirlwind to drop it in the gutter by the window. But they will be carrying the rope, which is a clumsy thing. Oh dear, how complicated. I will have to make a bundle of the rope and suit. Whirlwind and Gale can carry it in turns. Then they will have to separate the two. Dear, dear. I will make a bag with two handles to make it easier. The wetsuit will have to be dumped at the beach and Sammy's clothes dropped near here.

" Yes. This is where all you seagulls can be really useful. Sammy will have a sweater – most important – at least a shirt and shorts, socks and shoes – the shoes could be left behind.

"Now, Sammy has to get to the coast, somehow, and from

what I hear, it's quite a long way off, and it must all happen before it's properly light. If he is comfortable flying with you eagles, do you think you could carry him there? I don't like the idea of him walking. He could easily be recaptured."

Whirlwind glanced at Gale and nodded. "It should be all right. We might have to rest once or twice."

"Now, Zabaduk seems to know the way to the coast and has met the dolphins. He can fly straight there and explain to Sammy about the wetsuit and prepare the dolphins to meet Sammy. They know my little harbour and can certainly take Sammy there, but it's a long way. He will need food and rest over at least one night. And he must not get too cold. You seagulls, if I made up some little parcels of food could you prepare a dump about half way along the coast? You will need to keep an eye on the dolphins and Zabaduk and show them and Sammy where it is.

"Finally, all going well, everyone will arrive at my little harbour. The best way for Sammy to get up here would be for Whirlwind and Gale to carry him again. So you two eagles, when you have left Sammy with the dolphins, please bring the rope back!

"Now I must try to get a message to Giaccomo. Sammy's parents must be in a dreadful state. I hope I can give them some comfort, but I can't imagine what they can be persuaded to believe. Giaccomo will have to do the best he can."

⸺≋⸺

Poor Sammy and Zabaduk were having a very boring time while their excited friends were having all the fun of making preparations. Robin, Percy and Pickles paid them visits whenever they could manage to leave their precious nests, and the two of them carried out what Sammy called "exercises" trying to improve their understanding of each other's "talk". They gradually made up a sort of picture code, a kind of dictionary, so that Sammy would cry out "breakfast" and imagine boiled eggs and toast.

As Zabaduk could not make noises, he drew Sammy's attention with his trigger image of himself flying over the cliffs. Then he would imagine Robin on the windowsill and Sammy would call out "Robin!" Of course it did not always work, but they could nod or shake their heads to show whether they agreed or not. They slowly improved and easy thoughts could be shown quite quickly, sometimes, to Sammy's surprise, faster than by talking.

Then very early one morning when they had almost given up there came a tap on the window and a croak. Zabaduk, who never really slept (although he could get very tired after flying) called out: "Is that you, Breezy?"

"Yes," came the reply in the almost dark. "We're ready to go! You must wake up Sammy. Titch and I will be bringing up a rope. Whirlwind and Gale will lift Sammy to the ground. You must explain to him that he needs to wind a loop around his chest from the middle of the rope so that the eagles can lift him from both ends. They will carry him all the way to the coast, but will probably need to take a rest along the way."

"OK, I'll do my best but our conversations have to be very simple. Here goes!". Zabaduk, who was next to the sleeping boy gave him a prod with his nose. It took quite a while to wake Sammy but eventually he stirred and growled "Shut up, Zabby, it's not morning yet."

"Oh yes it is," muttered Zabaduk and went on prodding and imaging himself flying over the cliffs.

Suddenly Sammy really woke up in excitement.

"Oh Zabby, are we going?" he cried.

Zabaduk brought up a picture of the eagles holding a rope by both ends.

"Wow, do you really mean eagles?" said Sammy.

Zabaduk nodded, close against Sammy so that he could feel it, and imagined Sammy dangling from a loop in the middle of the rope.

"I have to wrap myself in the middle?" asked Sammy.

Zabaduk nodded again and spoke to Breezy:

"I think he understands, bring up the rope!"

There was a flutter of wings at the open window and soon another croak, rather muffled. By this time Sammy had realised what was happening and was ready and dressed as Breezy and Titch landed with a loop of the rope in their strong beaks.

"Great! Thanks, Oh thanks!" cried Sammy and took the middle of the rope from them. He was quick to see that they had brought up the middle, ready for him to wrap around himself, which he did without too much trouble. He had his sweater on since it was quite chilly.

"Tell him to keep the rope tight under his arms and hold on with both hands," said Breezy, "and climb out on to the gutter!" Leaving Zabaduk to interpret as best he could he and Titch flew off to warn the eagles.

It was getting light now, enough to make it quite easy for Sammy to clamber over the windowsill, hanging on to the rope. Although the ground was all in shadow, there was enough light in the sky for Sammy to see the huge eagles rising above the dark trees. He was almost overcome with wonder at the sight. Then he felt tugs at the rope and grasped it as tight as he could. He felt the rope getting tighter and tighter round his chest and then suddenly he was in the air! It was an amazing feeling to find himself swinging with the faint breeze in his face.

Zabaduk had been unable to explain to Sammy that the eagles were taking him all the way to the coast. Expecting to be deposited on the ground he was surprised to find himself soaring higher and higher into the rosy sky. Then he glimpsed something alongside. Turning his head he laughed to see Zabaduk. The dragon seemed to be laughing too. As he turned his head towards Sammy, his mouth was open and his long red tongue was whirling around. He looked surprisingly graceful with his long wings fully opened, making big slow sweeps. All of a sudden Zabaduk closed his wings and dived, opening them again under Sammy and swooping up again, flapping his way up on the other side.

"Brilliant!" cried Sammy. He could see more and more of the countryside as the sun rose. He saw the coast in the distance and thought he could see splashes which might be the dolphins. Far above his head he saw the great eagles winging their way with the ends of the rope in their talons. I'll never forget this, he thought.

Then he felt the eagles starting to glide down. They were some distance still from the sea and Sammy wondered what was happening. Near the ground they slowed and with short flaps of their wings lowered Sammy near Zabaduk who had landed first. The dragon imagined a picture of Sammy asleep in bed.

"Oh, they must be tired," exclaimed Sammy, and indeed the eagles seemed to be taking deep breaths.

"Won't you introduce me?" asked Sammy.

"This is Whirlwind, Merlin's friend and lookout," said Zabaduk, nodding towards the great bird and imagining leaves whirling in the wind.

"Whirlwind?" asked Sammy cautiously.

Zabaduk and Whirlwind nodded and the eagle flapped his wings.

"Thank you so much for helping me escape," said Sammy. "It really was an amazing experience. One I shall never forget. And this must be your mate?"

This time Zabaduk imagined a rough sea and sailing boats. It took longer for Sammy to guess the right name, but he got there eventually to the eagles' delight.

Then the eagles flapped their readiness to go and Sammy tightened his loop and hung on tight as he was lifted into the air again. Next time they dropped him on the beach, where he found Zabaduk with Breezy and Titch accompanied by what seemed to be a crowd of seagulls, all hopping about excitedly. Nearby was a strange bundle which Breezy pushed towards him. Sammy examined it and realised it as a wetsuit which he had seen surfers wearing.

"What a clever idea! I wonder who thought of that?"

He saw one of the seagulls he recognised as Titch bouncing up and down.

"You, Titch? Well done!" he said, and began to take all his clothes off. The sun was now quite high in the sky and it was getting warmer quickly, but he shivered in the faint breeze as he sorted out how to put on the suit. Although it was a little big for him, it was still difficult to pull on, tight as it was around his body. Finally he stood there on the beach feeling quite grown-up, although at the same time he was a little scared and shivery inside now, at the thought of swimming out to sea with only the strange dolphins to keep him from drowning.

Zabaduk could feel Sammy's doubts and gave him as much encouragement as he could. He took off and flew around him, calling at the same time to the seagulls who also flew up excitedly. Then the dragon flew off to fetch the dolphins. He found them not far off shore.

"Nosy!" he called, "Are you there? We're ready to go."

"Here I am," cried one of them, leaping and spinning out of the water. Zabaduk remembered the scar on his nose.

"Please come in as close as you can, especially whoever is carrying him first."

"That's me. We're ready for you. I'll come in close. What a lark!"

"He's wearing a special suit to keep warmer, but please don't let him get too tired or cold. When you feel it's time for a rest, bring him in to the shore. There is food for him around the coast. If it's not nearby, the seagulls will bring it. We'll all be keeping watch over you. Hope the weather stays fine!"

Zabaduk flew back and Sammy saw the dolphins approaching. Plucking up his courage waded out to meet them. When he was almost out of his depth, one of them came straight up and nudged him with a scarred nose.

"Nosy, meet Sammy," called Zabaduk from above, giving him a picture of a dolphin's nose.

"Nose? Nosy?"

The dolphin squealed and rolled over. Sammy laughed and felt much better. "That's easy to remember," he said and rubbed the dolphin's nose. Then, taking a deep breath he took hold of the dorsal fin and scrambled up behind. He realised that the dolphin's skin was quite rough and was glad of the suit protecting his bottom and legs. Nosy squealed again and turning carefully went out to meet his friends. They all moved along the coast with the whole group leaping and squealing around Sammy and Nosy. Suddenly Sammy realised where he was, riding the wonderful creature, no longer in imagination. He gave a great shout and let go the fin to throw his arms wide. This caused Nosy to give a leap in excitement and land with a big splash. Sammy had just time to grab the fin again as they both went under the water! It was only a brief ducking and Sammy came up laughing. Zabaduk keeping pace overhead did a swoop around them. Looking up, Sammy saw that the whole flock of seagulls were following too.

"Hi Breezy!" he called. "You up there somewhere?"

One of the seagulls detached himself from the flock and came swooping down too, giving a great squawk. Sammy felt reassured with all his friends keeping him company.

And so they proceeded around the coast. Every so often Zabaduk would call "Goodbye," flashing a signal for "rest", and make his way to the beach. After a while Nosy gave a double squeal and Zabaduk gave his "rest" signal again, with a picture of two dolphins. Sammy wondered what would happen next, but soon found out. Nosy slid down under the water and he found himself swimming! Then he felt another body coming up between his legs, lifting him up again and a different dolphin gave his squeal. This on had a chip on his fin and Sammy received a picture of a dolphin fin waggling.

"Hi, Finny," he cried, wondering whether the picture had come from Zabaduk or the dolphin. He decided there was no longer much difference and the dolphins were learning how to speak to him. The dolphin gave his squeal again, the picture fin waggling away.

Sammy lost track of time. They were swimming along at a good pace now. Dolphin steeds changed several times. The sun grew warm on his back, but after what seemed a long while, he felt himself growing tired, and his legs beginning to lose their feeling. The dolphin under him, who happened to be Nosy again, seemed to sense his tiredness. He gave three big squeals and turned towards the beach. Sammy slid off in the shallow water and waded to the shore. He really was tired and the suit felt cold and clammy. He decided to take it off and lay down in the sun.

My, that feels good, he had time to think before he felt his eyes closing.

⇒⇐

Holding Merlin's letter, Giaccomo gave a whoop. "Hooray!" he cried. "At last. I must get this to Eliza." He went to his telephone and not long after opened the door to her. "Read this!" he commanded. Aunt Eliza took the letter from him and read it in some wonder.

"Goodness gracious me," she said. "Dolphins! The child will be frozen, if he is not drowned first."

"I don't think so," replied Giaccomo, "see what he says about a wetsuit. He and his friends love a touch of drama, but Milo would not risk Sammy's life. But he describes his place of imprisonment in such a way that it could, perhaps be found. We can hope that Sammy is now free. Do you think the police should be told?"

They both thought hard.

"The most important thing is somehow to reassure his parents," said Aunt Eliza. "But how? They would never believe all this. As for the police, the house will surely be deserted by now, and I can't think it would help matters to have helicopters buzzing around the dolphins."

"No," said Giaccomo thoughtfully, "but what is worrying me is what the kidnappers will do next. I suspect that Maladok will send out his scouts – falcons. They may well find the expedition; from what I can imagine the dolphins will be accompanied by all the seagulls and should be clearly visible. He will report back to the kidnappers. What will they do, I wonder? I am sure they have no helicopters. But Sammy needs to come in to rest and eat. They will follow round the coast, I think, and lie in wait. Oh dear."

"I can only think of one thing to do," said Aunt Eliza, "We must go after them!"

"We?" said Giaccomo in horror. "What can we do? We are not police and really, I know you think yourself fit, but you are a woman, and I am an old man! We'll get ourselves shot, which won't help Sammy."

"Nonsense, you only pretend to be old, to help you sell toys, like the old toy maker in Pinocchio! We will be a couple on a holiday round the coast. We'll keep our eyes open, and if we see any danger, I will call up help on my new mobile phone." She waved it at Giaccomo, who looked a little mollified, but still rather scared.

"Bu - but what about Sammy's parents?" he stammered.

"I know. We'll leave it to Arthur. We'll tell him that we have heard that Sammy has escaped and that we are going to find him, and that we'll call him if we run into any trouble. We'll ask him to tell Sammy's parents but won't give him any details. That way they will be relieved and we won't have so much explaining to do."

Giaccomo looked doubtful but could suggest nothing better.

"We'll go tomorrow, early. Go and get yourself packed. We'll phone Arthur just before we go, so that he can't raise objections! Better still, we'll just leave a confidential message for him. Solicitors must be used to that."

⇒⇐

But Aunt Eliza was not the only one with a mobile phone. Towards evening when Sammy had made several trips Zabaduk, ever watchful, glimpsed two falcons circling high over their heads. He sent Titch off to Merlin to ask for help from Whirlwind. Long before reinforcements could arrive the falcons had disappeared.

Whirlwind had carried a bundle which proved to be a warm blanket, much to Zabaduk's relief. There was no longer a sun to warm Sammy. Good for Merlin and the eagles, he thought. When Sammy was too tired to continue that evening he wrapped himself thankfully in the blanket while he ate the food which had been left. He was so tired that he had barely time to finish his supper. Zabaduk did not mention the falcons to Sammy, but he warned the seagulls to keep half an eye open and hid himself among some rocks to keep watch.

The night passed peacefully, but next day they were all alert. Sammy awoke cold and did not venture into the sea until the sun had risen and warmed him thoroughly, but soon he was enjoying the playful journey with the dolphins leaping around and under him. One or two tried leaping over him and Nosy but the leader put a stop to this after a near collision. Then, looking up, Sammy saw two tiny black specks circling very high up. Zabaduk had seen them too. Too high for me, he thought, but suddenly they seemed to fall sharply out of the sky and diving after them was the huge form of Whirlwind.

That's more like it, thought Zabaduk, and started flapping his way up to join the fight. But long before he got near, the falcons, who could fly very fast, had sped away out of danger and disappeared.

I wonder if they are there as guides, thought Zabaduk, and flew in to the shore to have a look. Sure enough he saw some movement among the rocks. As he flew nearer he recognised their old captors gazing out to sea, where the dolphins and Sammy could just be made out. Then the man looked up and he saw the look of amazement and fear on his face. Suddenly the man held up a pistol and fired. Zabaduk felt a kind of tearing noise where a bullet zipped through his tail. A great surge of anger came over him at this man who had captured him and his friend and imprisoned them. He dived straight at him and hit him on his head, so hard that he knocked him over. The woman was waving her hands over her head and running towards a car on the road above. The man scrambled to his feet and followed her. Safely inside with the windows up they scowled at Zabaduk who flew around them. Eventually they seemed to realise that Sammy was safe from them, for the time being at least, and drove off.

Some distance away, hidden behind some bushes, Aunt Eliza and Giaccomo watched the fight in amazement. As the kidnappers drove off Zabaduk made a final circle and spotted Aunt Eliza waving at him. He flew over to them and landed nearby.

"Well done, Zabby!" cried Aunt Eliza. "Are you hurt?" Zabaduk found he could pick up her feelings well, but wondered how he could reply. He imagined a stream of balloons rising in the sky, hoping she would understand his pride and joy at driving off the kidnappers.

"Balloons!" she said. "Yes, I understand you, Zabby, you wonderful dragon, but did you get shot?"

Giaccomo knelt down and inspected him.

"What wonderful wings! They don't seem damaged, but you have a hole through your tail. Eliza, do you have any sewing things? I could patch this up."

Aunt Eliza looked in her handbag.

"Only a small needle and thread. Will this do?" she said holding them up.

Giaccomo took them gratefully. "I'll just put in a wee stitch to prevent any tearing," he said. "There, that should do." He got back to his feet and Zabaduk took off. He circled around them once, waggling his wings to say thank you and went back to make sure Sammy was all right.

"Well, that was very instructive," mused Giaccomo, gazing out at Sammy and the dolphins, circled by Zabaduk and the flock of seagulls. "I think we can safely leave them. They must be making their way to Merlin's hideout. But I think we must try to find it too. How is Sammy to get back?"

"Oh yes!" said Aunt Eliza. "I can't wait to meet Merlin. If we follow the coast, keeping them in sight, we won't go wrong."

"But what about the kidnappers? asked Giaccomo. They could do the same. Also I suspect they were found by Maladok's falcons."

"I have written down the number of their car," said Aunt Eliza. "And the man has a pistol. I think it's time to bring in the police. We can simply say we saw the man firing his pistol at something or someone. They should arrest them for that. And I bet they find other things to charge them with, or the Italian police will."

She phoned Arthur and told him that they had seen Sammy, who was safe and being escorted to Merlin's home, where they intended to pick him up. Then she told him about the kidnappers having a pistol and gave him the number of the car. Arthur was fascinated and promised to get the police on to them as soon as he could, and to ring back with any news.

And so Giaccomo and Aunt Eliza drove slowly along the coast road. Every so often the road went inland, but when they got back to the sea again they could always pick up the convoy by the covering flock of seagulls. Eventually they came in sight of the lone mountain. But when they came to its foot they found themselves at a sheer cliff face and could see no way up!

※

By the third day Sammy was quite brown. Although his suit protected him from the sun as well as the cold, he spent a lot of time on the beach without any clothes on, getting warm and resting. Quite often, if it had been a long ride, he was so tired that he slept in the sun. He felt much stronger, too. As he got to know the dolphins and they grew used to him, they sometimes played games in the sea. Nosy, or whoever was playing steed, would roll over and tip him into the sea. Then they would swim around and he would catch a dolphin by the tail and be dragged along for a bit. He learned to keep his face out of the water so that his chest raised a huge spray. Sometimes they pulled him under the water, but always gave a whistle first so that he had time to take a deep breath. He found he could hold his breath longer and longer. When the pulling dolphin felt him struggling he would shoot to the surface and right out of the water so that Sammy flew through the air, gasping, before diving in again.

Towards midday he saw a mountain rising, so it seemed, from the sea. As they grew closer he could see two eagles circling over the peak. I wonder if we have arrived, he thought. Sure enough the dolphins closed in towards a jetty where he could see Zabaduk waiting for him, surrounded by the seagulls. There were steps leading down and, after Nosy had tipped him off, he swam to them and climbed up.

"Wow, we seem to have arrived," he said to Zabaduk. Then he turned to his dolphin friends and shouted to them all:

"Thank you, thank you, it has been wonderful!"

The dolphins squealed their welcome noise and gave a display of leaps while Sammy waved and waved. Then they turned and disappeared out to sea.

"I wonder if we'll ever see them again," he said to Zabaduk. "I seem to have been with them for ever."

Zabaduk drew his attention to his old clothes and the rope lying along the jetty. He took off the wetsuit for the last time and excitedly put on his clothes. Then he found the middle of the rope again and wrapped it around him. The seagulls rose in a squalling cloud as the two eagles, who had been watching everything from far above, glided down and picked up the ends of the rope. Once again Sammy found himself rising in the air, this time over the jetty, the beach and the sea. Far away he caught a glimpse of white spray where the dolphins were playing their game of tag. The mountain grew closer and he could see a robed figure with a white beard standing on what looked like a shelf or plateau with a large black cave opening further back. Zabaduk was curled up at his feet. A row of birds including some seagulls could also be seen at a respectful distance from the old man. Then they were gliding down and Sammy felt a pang of apprehension as he was lowered in front of Merlin. This was the Great Magician known only to his toys and friendly creatures. How should he, a boy invading his private hideout, behave? And how would he be received?

He was soon relieved by the smile of welcome on the old man's face.

"Hello Sammy, I have been looking forward to meeting you," said Merlin, holding out an old, gnarled hand. Sammy smiled in return as he shook it.

"Come, it must be tea time," said Merlin. Sammy saw that near a cave opening was an old building like a shepherd's croft set back against the cliff. There were other buildings like workshops along the bottom of the cliff. Merlin led the way into the croft and Sammy gazed at the rows of toys on the shelves. What a wonderful place, he thought, and how great to spend your life making toys.

"I did some baking this morning in preparation," said Merlin. "I don't know about you, but I love tea best of all. The best thing I found about England after I arrived here – I came from Italy, you know." He handed Sammy a large and still warm doughnut. "Raspberry jam inside, my favourite," he smiled. "I'm not much of a cook really. I cook things I like, and whatever the birds catch for me. But I tend to stick to fruit juice," he added handing Sammy a mug.

Sammy, biting into the doughnut and licking the fresh jam around his lips, thought he was the greatest cook.

Merlin spread a scone with jam for himself. "One of the problems with living up here is butter," he continued. "It's amazing what one can do with fish oil, but fish margarine does not go with jam.

"I have heard that there is a car at the foot of my mountain," he continued. "Zabaduk has gone to have a look, as I think it may be your Aunt Eliza."

"Do you know Aunt Eliza? said Sammy in surprise. "Sorry," he apologised as crumbs flew across the table.

"Well, I have not yet had the privilege of an introduction," said Merlin, "but I can't help knowing all about her from Zabaduk and all your bird friends. We have to get you home, somehow, you know. The problem is that there is no road up. Luckily, as I would have been invaded years ago."

"But how did you get up here?" asked Sammy, trying to imagine Merlin being lifted by an eagle.

"No, no eagles," said Merlin with another smile. "The mountain is almost hollow, as I discovered when I first arrived. It is honeycombed with passages, one of them ending up on this shelf. I have not explored them for years. I do not know if I could find my way down to guide them up. I will have to try, I think. If all else fails, Whirlwind can carry you down. But I know that Eliza is longing to meet me, and I would love to see my old friend Giaccomo again, if he is with her, as I suspect."

Sammy was wondering about his imagined picture. "Did you know I was thinking of you being carried up by eagles?" he asked.

"Of course," said Merlin. "Just as I think you must have seen something of the passages in the mountain, and probably Aunt Eliza's car! Zabaduk has told me you are getting pretty expert at telepathy – that's what some grown-ups call this way of talking."

"Wow," said Sammy thoughtfully. He took a drink from the mug. It tasted like squashed raspberries.

"Sorry if it's too much raspberry," said Merlin. "But it is still the season. I have a garden round the mountain towards the South," he added in response to Sammy's unspoken question. Sammy was beginning to find Merlin's reading of his thoughts rather disconcerting.

"Can I go with you inside the mountain?" he asked, changing the subject.

"Perhaps," said Merlin. "But it will be tiring. It's a long way down, and we may get lost."

Just then Zabaduk flew in. Sammy caught pictures of Aunt Eliza and a man he thought must be Giaccomo.

"As I thought," said Merlin. "Tell you what. I will send a message to Eliza to wait, and that we may not reach her till morning. I suppose she must have a tent or something. You, Sammy, will go to sleep now, soon as you can, and we'll try to find our way overnight. The passages will be dark anyway. And Zabby can come with us. The darkness makes no difference to him, you see. He will guide us! Of course I will bring what light I can."

⇛⇚

"Oh bother!" said Aunt Eliza as she read the note that Titch had dropped at her feet. "Merlin must think we have camping equipment. Perhaps we should have brought some. We wouldn't have had such trouble finding the dolphins in the morning. What shall we do? I don't think there is a hotel or B&B for miles. I don't fancy sleeping in the car much."

Giaccomo had been looking at the cliff face. "There simply has to be an entrance somewhere, you know. Merlin must have got up when he first arrived, and he's no mountaineer. Let's have a look around. There may be a cave where we can shelter." He started to walk along the edge of the cliff and Aunt Eliza ran to catch him up. Suddenly he looked down at the ground.

"Here, look! Unless I am much mistaken these are bat droppings. They are most crowded over here." He went up to the cliff and looked hard, feeling around above the spot where the droppings were most numerous. He found a small crack in the rock which the bats may have been using, but it was too small for humans. He put his hand in and felt around. His fingers found a smooth piece of rock that seemed to fit his hand, and pulled. To their astonishment a huge boulder seemed to split from the cliff!

Carefully pulling, Giaccomo was able to move one side of the boulder to leave a space big enough for a man or woman to squeeze through. The boulder was so closely fitting that, without help from the bats, they would never have found it. The two of them stepped away and gazed at the doorway they had discovered.

"This must be ancient," said Giaccomo. "Do we have a torch?"

Aunt Eliza ran excitedly back to the car and carried back a large lantern torch. She handed it to Giaccomo.

"Here, I have changed wheels with this. I always keep a fresh battery in it. You go in first. It may be full of bats, which are not my favourite creatures! And be careful, the air may be bad."

Giaccomo squeezed himself through the doorway and switched on the torch, sniffing the air which seemed quite fresh. He found himself in a large cavern. It was so big that he could not make out the far end, or the ceiling. But it was surprisingly warm. There were no bats visible although he was aware of one that seemed to come in, squeak, and disappear. He poked his head back through the doorway and called Aunt Eliza to come in. They spent some time looking around.

"It must be an old cavemen's home," said Aunt Eliza. I hope there are no ghosts!"

"Don't be silly," said Giaccomo. "Just be thankful there are no bats here. They must have made their home further in. We can look around some more, but mustn't get separated. There is only the one torch. And we need to save the battery. We need to be sure, too, that we can always see the doorway. There should be enough light for that even at night. I don't suppose you have any oil in your shopping bag?"

"Strangely, I do," said Aunt Eliza. "I bought a small bottle of olive oil which I needed at home."

"Excellent!" said Giaccomo. "We can improvise an oil lamp. My pipe cleaners should help. Let's do it now, while it's still light. Then we can put down some bedding and explore a bit."

They set to work to make an oil lamp out of an old bottle and a wick. The pipe cleaner did not work too well but Aunt Eliza found some cotton tape which did the trick. Inside the cavern it gave enough light, with the open door, to help them lay down heaps of bracken and soon they had quite a snug bedroom. Then they took up the torch once again and walked slowly around the wall – more properly the edge of the cavern. They found lots of things the old cavemen had left behind – flint tools, some pots and even what may have been a primitive lamp, but it smelled of rancid fat and they left it alone. Moving away from the wall a little, they found the remnants of what must have been the fireplace, with charred wood and animal bones. Further along the wall they came across some beautiful paintings.

They spent so much time exploring that they found the light in the doorway fading.

"I say, I'm quite hungry," said Giaccomo eventually. "Let's get that bottle of wine and the bread and salami we bought. I suppose we could make a fire, but I don't feel cold and don't feel much inclined to gather firewood."

"Oh do let's!" said Aunt Eliza. "We would feel just like the old cavemen."

So they went out again into the evening and gathered a great pile of dry branches which they arranged in the old fireplace and lit with the help of a little more oil. Then they sat around on some old logs which must have been primitive seats and ate and drank by the light of the fire. It seemed just the place for story telling and Giaccomo found himself telling Aunt Eliza old children's stories from Italy.

"This must be just how they used to spend their evenings," said Aunt Eliza after one of Giaccomo's tales. "Perhaps they are all around us listening!" They grew silent and listened for a while, everything seemed peaceful, there was no sound, nor any ghosts.

When they grew tired they went back to their beds and blew out the light from the oil lamp. As Giaccomo had thought, with the door open it was not completely dark. They put on all the clothes they had and tucked themselves inside the bracken. They were soon asleep.

≡≡

Zabaduk hopped and flapped ahead of Merlin and Sammy down the tunnel. It was dark as the darkest night, but it never worried him and he led the way with confidence. The passage led onwards and downwards and seemed to be in a large spiral. Every so often they would stop for Merlin to mark the wall with a round splodge of luminous paint. He, at least, had to find the way back home! They stopped mostly where branch tunnels led off towards the interior – or so it seemed. Merlin carried a home-made torch of burning sticks and cloth which had been dipped in a mixture of resin from the pine trees and fish oil. It gave out a bright light, but they could not see far into the darkness. He passed it to Sammy when he was busy painting. Sammy carried a lantern with a candle, but it was not lit. They kept it for emergencies.

After a long descent they emerged into a huge cavern, so high that it was impossible to see any roof.

"This must be the main vent of the volcano," said Merlin. "That's what my mountain is, of course, a very old, and hopefully quite extinct, volcano. But the hole at the top fell in long ago, which is why it's so dark. My cave, where we started, must be a smaller vent. But where do we go from here, I wonder? I think I must have found my way up by accident. I will put a big splodge here, to show the way back. I can make out quite a number of passages leading out of here. How to find the right one?"

Just then they heard a squeak and a rustle of wings.

"Bats! Wonderful. Let's see if they can show us the way." He gave quite a good imitation of the squeak and called:

"Hello bats! Can you hear me. I know you can't see who I am behind all this fire, but it's me, Merlin!"

There was a chorus of squeaks and a whole flock seemed to be flapping around them, keeping well away from the burning torch.

"Sorry, bats, I'll put the torch out and use the lantern. Here Sammy, pass it to me."

After lighting the candle from the torch, Merlin thrust the torch into a convenient crevice and rubbed it around until it went out. The lantern gave much less light but did not seem to disturb the bats who came closer.

"Hello, Merlin," called one of the bats. "I'm Betty. We have been hoping for ages that you would come back and see us again. Of course none of us can remember you directly, but we pass all the stories we can hear about you on to our children. Are you lost again?"

Zabaduk saw a strange picture of the inside of the mountain with passages everywhere, and passed it to Sammy.

"I remember now! You helped me when I first arrived here. You led me to my home! Thank you, Betty. How could I have forgotten. And I'm sorry that it has been so long. Now we need to find the way out at the bottom, to find some friends. Have you seen another man and a woman anywhere? They may be just outside."

"Oh no, they are sleeping in the large cavern at the entrance. Follow us!"

It was not so easy to follow them. Zabaduk could manage it and Merlin suggested painting his tail with luminous paint.

"No, no!" said Zabaduk. "Paint my tongue! It will look like fire."

"But we can't see your tongue," answered Merlin. "Come here, I'll do your tongue, but I must put a spot on the ends of your wings and tail so that we can follow you."

So Zabaduk followed the bats through one of the tunnels, and Merlin and Sammy followed the glowing spots and the bright tongue which flew out every so often. Merlin did not forget to mark the entrances of the tunnels. Eventually they entered the big cavern and saw the two bundles of bracken. Aunt Eliza and Giaccomo were still asleep, but the dawn was just breaking and visible through the open door. The noise of their entrance and the squeaking of the bats woke the two sleepers, who emerged, looking up at them in relief and joy. They all walked out into gathering day.

"Aunt Eliza!" cried Sammy, hugging her with tears of relief. "Oh, I've had such an adventure, but it's so good to see you again. I did wonder, sometimes."

"Believe me, Sammy, We've all wondered too! We've not even told your Mummy and Daddy very much. They do know at least that I've come to look for you." She looked around and saw Merlin hugging Giaccomo.

"It's been a long time, old friend," said Merlin.

"Hasn't it just!" replied Giaccomo.

When they broke off, Sammy took Aunt Eliza by the hand and brought her to Merlin.

"Aunt Eliza, this is my friend Merlin."

And so, Aunt Eliza's dream was fulfilled. But she and Giaccomo could not be content with introductions outside the mountain.

"Please, do let us visit your home before we leave," they asked.

Merlin sighed. "Of course you are both very welcome," he replied, but it's a long way up and down, and probably too much for Sammy and Zabaduk. I'll have to go up anyway, but these two could really do with some sleep. It's been a long night for them. Sammy probably needs to sleep for a week. Let's all have a rest while Sammy tells you all his adventures, though I'm sure you know a lot already, then I'll say my good-byes to the young ones and take you up. Have you got a good torch? I have marked all the entrances to the tunnels, but you will need to be careful finding your way down. If you get lost, Zabby will come to fetch you. He knows how to follow the bats, who will always know where you are."

And so that's what they decided. Sammy was already half asleep and was very glad to bury himself in Aunt Eliza's bracken bed. But before he did so he had to find out what had happened to the kidnappers.

"Oh, I had a call from Arthur earlier today," said Aunt Eliza. "I had told him about the pistol the man fired at Zabaduk and the police found them and arrested them. It seems they are well known to the Italian police who have been looking for them. You are not the first they have kidnapped! Anyway they are locked up out of harm's way and should be sent to Italy for trial."

"Good!" said Sammy and Zabaduk together.

While Sammy slept, Zabaduk kept watch and had a running commentary from Betty about the progress of Aunt Eliza and Giaccomo. They became good friends. In the end, Merlin's careful marking of the route proved enough for the two to find their way down, after a long talk with Merlin over lunch. Although Merlin was very tired, Aunt Eliza helped with the cooking. They left him to his bed after the meal and went back down through the mountain. When they came to the central cavern, they could see the helpful bats crowding around the right exit.

It was early evening when they set off home, and they did not reach Sammy's house until long after his bedtime.

But nobody cared.